I0533891

THE
RUDDERHAVEN
SCIENCE FICTION AND FANTASY ANTHOLOGY
IV

Edited by

Douglas Rudder

RudderHaven
3014 Washington Ave
Granite City, IL 62040

Published by:
RudderHaven
3014 Washington Ave
Granite City, IL 62040
USA

First Softcover Printing, September 2016, RudderHaven
(ISBN 978-1-932060-20-1)

Edited by Douglas Rudder, Sheri Rudder, Becca Rudder, Jonathan Rudder, C. K. Deatherage
Cover Art and Design: Douglas, Sheri, and Becca Rudder
Nebula image Courtesy NASA/JPL-Caltech
Landscape image Courtesy Jon Sullivan/PDPhoto.org
Illustration in "A Sister's Path" by Sheri Rudder

Printed in the United States of America
ISBN 978-1-932060-20-1

Acknowledgements

Thanks to all of our authors, editors, and everyone who made this book possible, and to our families and friends for their support and encouragement.

Special thanks to our readers. We hope you enjoy the characters, worlds, and stories we have presented to you. If our stories have sparked your imagination, touched your hearts, or tickled your sense of humor, then we count it a success.

Contents

A Cold Autumn Night

Jonathan M. Rudder

A furious wind blasted down upon the darkened landscape as lightning struck and thunderclaps echoed through the grim night skies. There would be no sailing for the ships lying in harbor at the Shipyard of Ilkatar, for none could survive such a rough main as the Western Sea was that night. Not even the great warships of Bhoredan, renowned as the mightiest vessels in all of Milhavior, could sail through that raging torrent.

Tempests as terrible as that were not common to the region, and the folk of the fishing villages spread along the coast of Ilkatar believed that they augured of ominous things, such as the Plague which ravaged the lands of Milhavior for nigh unto sixteen years. At one time, they had believed storms like these to be omens of pending doom from the sea-god, Heil. In later years, Heil and the other gods had been abandoned by all but a few of the

Ilkatari. Most had embraced the teachings of the Anal-etri, the Sea Elves, who served the Dawn King, Elekar.

Even so, the coast-dwellers remained somewhat wary of the unnatural, and this weather was anything but natural. Whether or not the mysterious beliefs of the Elves held any truth mattered little: the winds of this storm did indeed bear tidings.

"Ach! Like the very Winds of Hál these be!"

The elderly man turned his greying face away from the window of his workplace in the Shipyard's kitchens and moved back to the small table at the center of the room.

Gwydnan was only a simple kitchenhand, though he could have been mistaken for the Shipyard's Master by the elegance of his raiment: a handsome, white tunic and black waistcoat, with sable trousers to match, and shiny, black leather boots, apparel not common to men of his lowly position. This, combined with his neatly-combed, snow-white locks—thinning though they were— and the chiseled wisdom of his face, made him appear more a stately gentleman than a hardened commoner.

He had been, at one time, a man of high position at the Shipyard. Only recently had he been assigned to work in the kitchens. Before the sudden change in status, he had served nearly twenty-six years at the docks as the Chief Dockmaster's assistant, having begun his employ at the Shipyard at a self-proclaimed age of sixty-three . . . though it was generally agreed that he was much older. He was, of course, greatly put out by his apparent demotion to kitch-enhand, but there was nothing to be done about it, and he well understood that. There were other responsibilities attached to his change in position to which he was more suited than any of the rough hands at the docks.

Kanstanon, a lad of eleven summers, remained at the window watching the raging storm with curious, brown eyes. The child's hand-me-down tunic, also a muddy brown color, was a bit too large for his slight figure.

A tremendous thunderclap shattered the air, rattling the window pane and startling the boy. Several bright bolts of lightning split the sky, tracing jagged, blue lines across the boy's vision. Kanstanon backed away from the window and joined his master at the table, sliding into a chair across from Gwydnan.

"Master, what is Hál?" he asked. He was enthralled with tales of mysterious places and things, and the Winds of Hál sounded very mysterious to him.

The old man looked at the boy with a brow cocked.

Kanstanon believed his master often enjoyed satisfying his inquisitive mind, but he could never be sure, for Gwydnan always put on a weary frown when asked a question.

As the boy anticipated, Gwydnan grimaced and testily replied, "Come now, Kanstanon, have you learned nothing? Or have you slept through all your lessons?"

"Oh no, Master," Kanstanon quickly replied, thinking his master only playing at being vexed. Still, he had to be careful. "But you haven't never taught me nothing about Hál. I heard Master Roby and Master Tasic mention it a lot, but what they said didn't make any sense."

"You never mind what they were talking about. If either of them said anything about Hál, you can be certain it was well out of context," Gwydnan told the boy. "And, yes, I have taught you about it, though I may not have referred to it by that name. Tell me, what are the Three Spheres?"

"The Three Spheres make Ona Orilal, the Great Sphere of the World," Kanstanon answered with a proud grin . . . which promptly vanished when his master waived his reply.

"Yes, yes, that's very nice, but it is not what I asked you. Perhaps, I should rephrase my question. What are the *Realms* of the Three Spheres?"

Kanstanon knew that his master was truly perturbed now. He bit his lip thoughtfully, drilling through his lessons in his mind. Finally, when he believed he knew the desired answer, he put voice to his thoughts. "The First Sphere is Alaren Orilal, the High Realm, ruled by Elekar, the Dawn King. There, the Alara and other immortals of the Dawn dwell also."

Kanstanon glanced at his master, but Gwydnan's expression had not yet changed. He hoped that he had not left something out. He continued, this time thinking everything out very carefully. "The Second Sphere is En Orilal, the Mortal Realm. Here dwell the Free Kindreds: Men, Dwarves, Elves, and Saereni. The Elves are the only immortals among the Free Kindreds, and the Saereni have not yet been revealed to the other Kindreds.

"Some beasts of Darkness also dwell here: Kubruki, Trolls, Dragons, Drolar, and Jaf." His brown eyes darted to his master again, and this time the elder was nodding his approval.

Elated by this, Kanstanon went on a bit more enthusiastically. "The Third Sphere is Maelen Orilal, the Under Realm, ruled by Machaelon, who is also called Thanatos, the Deathlord. There, the Dark Alara and other immortals and beasts of Darkness dwell.

"These Spheres combined form Ona Orilal, the Realm Complete," he ended.

Gwydnan gave Kanstanon a proud smile and pointed a finger at him, playfully poking the boy's nose. "The Third Sphere is the answer to your question, lad. 'Tis called Hál in my native tongue, and by most here on the mainland.

"You will need to remember that when you are come of age, lad, for someday En Orilal shall have to face the Winds of Hál, the Storm of Death's Legion, when the Black Gates of Maelen Orilal open and the Deathlord returns to this world."

Kanstanon now understood a little as to what the Winds of Hál were. The Great Prophecies of the Third Age told that Thanatos would come into En Orilal to conquer the Second Sphere, and that his Shadow would be as the winds of a great storm, sweeping over the lands of the Mortal Realm. Only the return of the Heir of Ascon, the lost High King, would hold any hope for the world in that day, for Elekar's prophecies told that only by Ascon's hand would Machaelon be defeated.

The stableboy was awed and more than a little frightened by the thought. But he abandoned his wonder and reached a hand towards his master as Gwydnan's outstretched arm dropped to the table. The old man leaned forward a little, as though under a weighty burden, every breath becoming more difficult. Soon, his breathing became normal again, and total silence fell.

"Are you all right, Master Gwydnan?" Kanstanon asked in alarm.

The man did not answer him, but straightened in his seat. He sat in complete silence, rubbing his chin with a gnarled and sinewy hand. One small lamp spilled a dim glow over the table, glinting in the man's unblinking eyes.

Though his gaze was focused in the direction of his ward, Kanstanon knew that the old man did not see him. Kanstanon was no more to him at that moment than a speck upon a wall.

The child sat there in bewilderment, watching his master. The glow of the lamp softened the man's features, driving the deep lines and shadows from his face. The longer Kanstanon stared, it seemed to him that age drained out of the old man's features. Gwydnan looked neither young nor old to the boy. He appeared the same, yet somehow different.

After a few minutes, Gwydnan's lids relaxed, all signs of his great age returning to him, heavier than before. A deep weariness fell upon him. He looked at Kanstanon and spoke. "Gather some food, lad. We shall have company this night."

The stableboy jumped up from his seat and hurried off to the pantries to do as he was told. He did not question his master, for he knew that Gwydnan had seen the visitor through a vision. He had suspected for many of his short years that there was more to Gwydnan than anyone knew, for he had witnessed many strange things in the presence of his master which to him seemed miraculous—sick horses suddenly becoming well, casks of flour that seemed never to empty—and he had often heard Gwydnan chanting quietly in a strange tongue in the privacy of his room.

Kanstanon nervously fumbled with honey-cakes and small loaves of bread—freshly baked that afternoon— sweet fruits and hunks of white cheese, and stuffed them into a basket. The boy hurried back to the front room, trembling with excitement.

When Kanstanon came back into the room, he saw his master sitting at the table, his right elbow propped on its hard surface, quietly staring at the kitchen's outer entrance as if expecting it to swing open at any moment. The boy's eyes slowly followed Gwydnan's gaze to the front door. A heavy silence, a nervous peace, blanketed the chamber.

All at once, a vortex of wind swept into the room as the door slammed open, and a man hobbled in, his dusty, grey cloak and white robes flapping in the gale. He swiftly shut the door behind himself, without the slightest effort, even with the force of the high wind blowing against him.

The visitor held in his right hand an oaken staff, and under his left arm, he bore a long, tin box. He carefully rested his rune-marked stave against the wall, then filled the seat which Kanstanon had only just vacated a few minutes before, setting the box on the table before the other man. The stranger drew back his travel-worn hood and smoothed out his flowing, white beard.

Kanstanon's eyes glided to the staff propped against the wall. The strange lettering etched around the head of the stick told him that this man was a Wizard, for his master had taught him the rune-letters of Holy Athor, a form used only by Wizards. The boy backed into a dim corner, fearful of coming nearer, his eyes locked onto the long-bearded stranger.

Gwydnan, however, regarded the newcomer in fond recognition. "It has been a long time, my friend, since you last sat in my presence."

The wanderer nodded slowly. "Aye, a long time, indeed."

The kitchenhand held the visitor's gaze in his own, the visionary light briefly returning to his eyes. "You have grown a little, Odyniec. When last we sat together it was as Master and Apprentice. Now, I no longer bear the staff, but you."

Kanstanon grew confused by his master's words. Master and Apprentice? Bearing the staff? The conversation that followed bewildered him all the more.

Gwydnan chuckled, settling back in his chair. "I remember my anger at being appointed such a young pupil. But I was hasty in my judgment. You have kept a pure heart through these last years and have nearly completed your time."

A light smile cracked Odyniec's aged features at the recollection. "Nay, Master, I am still the same rascal that you took under wing those many years ago! But now I am weary; the staff weighs heavily upon my heart. I long to return home to the Temple. I only hope that Zanyben shall call me back to take an apprentice soon."

"Aye, your time will come soon enough," the elder assured his old student. "Have patience, my friend. Even I am forced to wait for my final charge to be delivered."

The smile on Odyniec's lips faded. His grey eyes strayed to the box, then back to Gwydnan. He spoke again, his voice low. "Nay. The time has come, Gwydnan, old master. The time has come for the Bearer of the Flame to be revealed. That is my purpose here, as I am sure you knew before now."

The kitchenhand registered no surprise at his former student's declaration. "I thought as much. In our

8

work, casual visits are few and far between. Very well, Odyniec, where is he? When shall he come?"

"You must give the box to a certain young man named Brendys," the Wizard responded. "He is the son of a local Horsemaster . . . from Shalkan, I believe."

Gwydnan's brow wrinkled in confusion. "Brendys? Of Shalkan? Are you certain of this?"

"Then you know of him?"

"Know of him? I know the boy all too well," Gwydnan replied. "He does not serve our King. He cannot use it. The Flame would destroy him should he try!"

"Brendys of Shalkan," Odyniec repeated evenly. "Fear not for his ignorance, Gwydnan. Fanos Pavo shall see to that. Your only worry is to deliver the Flame safely to its Bearer. The Winds of Hál are stirring!"

He paused before going on. "It has come to me that this Brendys shall be making a journey to Hagan Keep early next summer; you are to pass it on to him then . . . Fanos Pavo has so decreed. Do you know the words to say?"

"Aye," Gwydnan replied with a sigh. "I was the first to speak them long ago, was I not?"

"Good! Then all is in readiness."

Gwydnan slowly nodded, then motioned a hand towards his ward. "Kanstanon."

The boy was startled at the calling of his name, for his confusion had subsided a degree, and he had become deeply interested in the two elder men's conversation. Kanstanon froze when Odyniec glanced towards him and smiled a little.

The Wizard breathed deep the scent of freshly-baked bread and gave a deep sigh. "Ah, me! But I cannot stay for supper," he announced, bringing quick relief to the boy. "I must be fast on my way! Farewell, Gwydnan. May Fanos Pavo keep you and yours."

The bearded man rose to his feet, taking his staff in hand, and shoved open the door, a blast of cold wind gusting into the room once more. When the door was shut and the Wizard gone, Gwydnan arose from his chair and returned to his place at the window to watch the storm-wracked Sea.

"Put the basket on the table, Kanstanon, and come here . . . the time has come for you to learn who your master is."

Jonathan M. Rudder is the author of *The Milhavior Chronicles*, the exciting five-book epic series that follows the tale of Brendys of Shalkan, Bearer of the Flame of Elekar. The story begins with book one: *Sharamitaro.*

A Sister's Path

S. L. Rudder

Enyri hit the ground flat on her back, her hazel eyes flying open. The edge of a sword pressed lightly against her throat.

"Yield?" rang in her ears as more of a command than a question.

"Yes, I yield," she gave a small sigh, "Again." The young Elfess flipped her golden bangs back out of her eyes after the sword had been drawn away. She grasped the wrist of the arm extended to her and pulled herself up off the forest floor. "How many losses is this by the way?" she asked as she brushed leaves from the back of her surprisingly short hair.

Alynniel laughed at her younger sister, her green eyes shining. "Do you mean today, or are we counting all of our battles?"

Thinking some questions do not deserve an answer, Enyri straightened her clothing, turned, and walked away.

Her opponent called after her, "You are not quitting now? We have only just begun to practice."

Enyri glanced back over her shoulder at her older sister, but did not stop as she moved to place her sword and shield on the weapons rack next to the practice field. "We have been at this since dawn," she said with a shake of her head. "It is now well past the nooning. I have other things to do besides continuing to let you beat me senseless."

"See, you prove my point. You need more practice." Alynniel tucked a stray golden curl behind her small pointed ear, her smile and eyes taunting her younger sister.

"You practice enough for both of us," Enyri replied with a lop-sided grin as she retrieved her cloak, bow, and quiver. She gazed off through the trees for the space of a few heartbeats. "I am joining Renthalas' company of patrol scouts this eve. They will be leaving at sunset, and I need to bathe and to change my clothing before then."

Alynniel placed her sword's point on the ground and leaned on its pommel. "I think you merely want to avoid another defeat."

"You may be right," Enyri agreed glancing at her sister. "But then again I may just not want to take the chance of besting you before I leave and having you plan your revenge the entire time I am gone."

Her thought shifting once again, Enyri's eyes strayed out into the forest. "There is something different about the 'Wood, not a feeling of danger, just something strange. Have you not felt it?" She turned back toward Alynniel.

"There is nothing that I have noticed." Alynniel closed her eyes as though she were listening intently, her

12

face slightly raised towards the overhead sun beaming its way into the clearing. She stood immobile for several moments, letting her thoughts range out through the trees. Finally, she opened her eyes and gave a slight shrug, having noticed nothing amiss. "When you spoke to Father, could he too sense this strangeness?" she asked, turning her eyes back on her sister.

Enyri shook her head as she answered, "No, he assured me that all seems well, but he did not dismiss my concerns. That is why he encouraged me to speak to Renthalas about joining his patrol. Mother says she has felt a disturbance, but that it is mainly centered round me, not the 'Wood."

"And you are sure you would rather wander aimlessly through the forest than allow me to improve your sword skills?" Alynniel asked as she moved to the well scarred pell at the edge of the clearing.

With a final wave and a shake of her head, Enyri left the field, the sound of her sister's sword striking wood ringing in her ears. She would never understand how Alynniel could find such enjoyment in constant weapons practice. There were so many other things of wonder to learn about.

Before the sun slipped out of sight behind the trees of the Tharonwood, Enyri was waiting beside Renthalas, Telorin's chief scout. Enyri studied the 'Wood beyond them. The gentle breeze ruffled her hair, which barely reached the top of her shoulder, and pulled at her loose tunic and full cloak.

Renthalas, for his part, was studying Enyri.

"You are sure your patrols have not reported anything out of the ordinary?" Enyri continued the discussion they had been having as they waited for the rest of the company to assemble.

"No, my lady. Other than a few creatures that have made their way into the Tharonwood from the wilds beyond, there has been nothing reported. I do agree with my Lord Telorin, your father. If you have sensed something this strongly, an extra patrol or two are more than warranted."

Turning to face Renthalas as he spoke, Enyri was surprised at the intensity of his gaze. She lowered her head under the pretense of checking her pack and equipment to hide the blush of surprise she felt warming her cheeks. For more years than she could count, long before Renthalas was named chief scout, she had been begging him to let her join him on patrol so that she might wander through the 'Wood to her heart's content. He would call her a tag-along, but was always willing to share his knowledge, lore, and time with her. It was very disconcerting to realize that Renthalas might not be thinking of her as a tag-along anymore.

The possible discomfort of the situation was averted when the rest of the scouts joined them, and the patrol took their leave as the 'Wood darkened towards the gloaming. Enyri was left to ponder on her own as the daytime sounds gave way to those of the night and they moved farther from Iniriand and deeper into the trees.

Enyri and the patrol worked toward the western edge of the 'Wood. They found nothing of consequence outside of one huge tarbigier nest that had somehow escaped notice, enabling it to reach gigantic proportions. The tarbigiers were large blue-green flying insects, similar in size to a mastiff dog. Their hive-like nests could devastate sections of the 'Wood, strangling out the trees and plants they attached it to. The tarbigiers preyed on small animals and birds and did not balk at attacking Elves or other travelers. The party of scouts, along with Enyri, had a pretty good fight on their hands before they had exterminated the brood, even with the size of the company.

For the next three days, the forest remained peaceful to all but Enyri. Ever so slightly, her feelings of unrest grew with each passing day, but not one of the scouts noticed anything out of the ordinary.

That evening, Enyri was sitting by the fire, poking coals with a long slender stick and gazing into the flames, when Renthalas joined her. She accepted the cup he offered her without taking her eyes off of the fire.

"We will be turning east in the morning." The chief scout took a sip from his own cup and gazed at Enyri's lovely profile. "I just received word that a pack of Vargs were spotted on the Tolathar border. We will need to make sure they do not find their way into the 'Wood."

Without looking up, Enyri nodded. "I will be making my way west," she stated. "West and perhaps north." She raised her stick up in the air, watching the fire at its end glow and flame. "There is something *calling* to me. I cannot explain it better than that. I simply feel the need to push on."

Renthalas gently took her arm and pulled it down until the burning stick was back in the fire. Removing it from her grasp, he took her hand in both of his. "Are you sure that you should go on by yourself?"

"I still feel no sense of danger in the 'Wood," she replied as she looked at his hands cradling her own. "I feel more a sense of urgency and purpose than danger. It is as if I am drawing near a place that I must reach. Oh, I cannot seem to explain how I feel, even to myself."

Renthalas raised Enyri's face with two fingers under her chin. Leaning forward slowly, he placed a soft, tender kiss on her lips. Looking into her surprised eyes, he smiled and said, "I too have been dealing with a feeling that is hard to explain. You just be sure to take good care of yourself. I could not bear it if anything happened to my little tag-along."

The young Elfess stared after him in confusion as he left her there by the fire, her thoughts and emotions both swirling. If it were not for the fact that she could still feel the warmth of his kiss, she would have believed that she had drifted off to sleep and dreamed the entire thing. Shaking her head to try and clear it, she slowly made her way to the blankets she had spread out earlier. Pulling her covers up to her chin, she curled on her side. It was many long minutes before she was able to close her eyes and sleep.

Waking early, Enyri readied her pack and rolled her blankets. She was still unsure of just what had happened the night before at the fire. By the time the sun rose over the forest canopy, she had convinced herself that Renthalas was only being kind to her. He simply felt responsible for her and worried over his tag-along.

The scout patrol also arose before dawn, readying for their trip to the eastern border of the Tharonwood. Renthalas moved near Enyri to bid her farewell. All of her deductions from the morning melted away when she looked into his eyes. Though the Elf did not embrace or even touch her, there was a look in his eyes that she had never seen before. It was a look that made her short of breath, caused her heart to beat just a little faster, and brought a blush to her cheeks.

Renthalas must have been pleased with what he saw in her eyes, for he gave her a huge smile as he signaled his patrol to move out.

"I want you to have this," he said as he handed her a dagger in a long boot sheath. "You never carry a sword, even though we both know you are more than capable with one. We have practiced with daggers enough that I know you are very good with one. This dagger is longer than most, but it will serve you well when needed. I will feel much better if you have this."

Enyri drew the dagger from its sheath and slowly turned it in her hands. It was long and slender, the point and double-edge both sharp beyond compare. It was truly a thing of beauty, the hilt most of all. Not overly elaborate, the hilt and cross piece were shaped like twining vines. Nestled in the gleaming silver were small amethysts, like purple berries.

Raising her eyes in wonder, she found that Renthalas was already moving to catch up with his patrol.

"Take care, my little tag-along," he called as he tossed her a piece of fruit. Enyri caught it and heard his laughter as he lightly ran to overtake the other Elves. They were all out of sight and hearing before she realized that she had failed to even wave, let alone speak before he left.

Taking a bite out of the fruit, she shook her head as she slowly chewed. She bent down and fastened the sheath to the outside of her right boot, then picked up her pack, quiver, and bow. The next time she saw Tharonwood's chief scout, there were a few things she would be wanting him to clear up.

All that day, Enyri moved westward through the 'Wood toward Thryn Pass. Before she reached the forest's edge, she came to a stop. She felt the urge to turn north. She took a few more steps in the direction of the pass, but felt almost as if something were pulling her back, calling her to come. It was nothing audible, more like a feeling or sense in the deepest part of her being. The strangeness she had been feeling in the 'Wood for so long was now stronger than it had ever been. There was no sense of danger connected to the call, no darkness or impending doom that she could feel at all. It was more like someone, or something, was calling her name without saying it aloud.

"Well," she said as she first looked up through the lace of tree branches, then around the trunks that surrounded her, "this *is* why I came out into the 'Wood. Time to find out what this is all about." She straightened her tunic and secured the straps to her pack and quiver. With a warm smile on her face, she checked to make sure her dagger was still snug in its boot sheath. Following your feelings is all well and good, but it pays to be prepared. With a quick nod at that thought, she headed north at a brisk pace.

By evening, many long, difficult miles from where she had started that morning, Enyri reached a point where the mountains between Thryn Pass and the Collester Hills jutted out into the edge of the forest. The "call" had been growing stronger as the day progressed, and was more powerful now than it had been at any other time during this whole adventure. It was growing most insistent.

Dropping her pack down beside her, Enyri studied the rocks and boulders that spilled out under the trees in a massive jumble. The urge to continue was almost overwhelming, but feeling the fatigue in her body, she knew she must stop. Much better to camp for the night, and then face whatever the rocks might hold when she was rested and had plenty of light.

While searching for a likely place to make camp, Enyri came across a set of tracks. The tracks were several days old, but they belonged to a bearak, a huge spawn creature. The beasts possessed the head, fur, and claws of a gigantic bear, but were thinner bodied, and travelled on their hind legs. They were vicious, bloodthirsty fighters who used those claws to tear their victims limb from limb. She had no desire to meet one of the awful creatures if she could help it. Making camp on the ground was out of the question if there was a chance a bearak was in the area.

Carefully, Enyri began studying the tree trunks around her. Soon she found what she sought. On the east side of one of the larger trees just a few yards from the edge of the 'Wood, barely visible even if one knew what to look for, was a thin blaze. Having spent so much time with the Elven scouts, Enyri knew that blaze meant there was a platform hidden high up in the branches above her. Grasping the limb just above her head, she swung up into the tree and began climbing toward the platform.

Before she had made it halfway to her goal, there was a tremendous roar below her and the tree began to shake violently. Throwing her arms around the trunk to keep from falling, Enyri looked down across her shoulder to find out what was attacking her sanctuary. There looking up at her was a nightmarish bearlike face, its lips pulled back and razor sharp teeth gnashing. An enormous bearak! The biggest that she had ever seen! The creature stood well over seven feet tall. The bearak's hand-like, clawed paws grasped the lower branches as it began pulling itself up after her.

Frightened and annoyed, but knowing the bearak's greater weight would not allow it to climb up into the slender, upper branches where the platform waited, Enyri continued climbing the best she could. Below her, the bearak was making good time climbing up the larger limbs. Enyri had no desire to attempt fighting the beast with just her dagger. She quickly climbed on toward the platform where she could use her bow. The swaying of the tree as the bearak sought to reach her making this a most difficult task.

Finally, attaining her goal, she dropped her pack, strung her bow, nocked an arrow, and prepared to draw. Because of a bearak's extremely thick hide and heavy muscling, even an Elven arrow would have trouble penetrating to a fatal spot. From years of study, Enyri was well aware of the spawn's most vulnerable points. Having it climbing the tree she was in was going to make hitting one of those spots extremely hard. Knowing that patience was not just a virtue at this point, but might be the difference between life and death, she drew her arrow back to her cheek and watched for her best opportunity.

The bearak, for its part, was doing nothing to help. It struggled to climb higher up the tree, its great forearms wrapped around the trunk, its hind feet scrambling for a hold on the increasingly small branches. All of which caused the tree to sway and jump.

Enyri took a spread-legged stance, as though on the deck of a ship, and relaxed her pull, waiting for that one chance to present itself.

When it realized it could climb no higher, the bearak worked itself up into a frenzy. It stood with one hind foot on a broken branch and the other leg wrapped around the trunk. Growling and snarling, it grasped two higher boughs and attempted to shake Enyri loose like a piece of ripe fruit.

Enyri worked with the roll of the platform, sometimes barely keeping her balance. She waited for a clear shot, just one!

Finally, there it was! The bearak threw back its head in a roar of hatred and rage, exposing the hollow at the base of its throat. Quicker than thought, Enyri drew her bow to its limit and the arrow streaked down at the spawn below her. It entered the creature's throat, angling down through its body. With a strangled howl of fury, the bearak fell from the tree and plummeted to the ground. The tree's surge as the spawn's great weight left it almost threw Enyri from the platform, nearly allowing the bearak to accomplish in death what it could not do in life.

Enyri sank to her knees and peered over the edge, down into the darkness, but she could see nothing in the underbrush. She was positive her shot had killed the bearak and felt no need to check the carcass before morning.

Reaction to the episode was setting in, and Enyri felt tired and weak as the excitement of the battle ebbed away. She unstrung her bow and laid it down beside her after easing back from the edge. Retrieving her pack, she pulled out her blanket and wrapped it around her shoulders. Scooting back, her legs curled to the side and her shoulder resting against the trunk, she fell into a fitful sleep.

Before dawn, Enyri gathered her possessions and prepared to continue her. Once she had everything stowed away and ready to travel, she reached down to check the dagger in her boot. It was not there! At some point during her escape last night the dagger must have been knocked free of the sheath.

As she glanced around the wooden platform, Enyri muttered to herself, "I have to find that dagger or I will have more to answer for than Renthalas does when next I see him."

She gave her surroundings a more thorough going over. The dagger was not in sight and there were just not any places for it to be hidden on the platform.

"It must have fallen free as I was climbing," she thought. "Nothing for it but to search the ground."

With agility and grace, she quickly made her way to the forest floor. Enyri took small notice of the bearak's carcass. She could see one leg sticking out from behind a shrub near a large boulder where the spawn had landed. The beast lay still as stone, and after a brief glance she forgot it was there.

As she turned her back on her late foe, she caught the glint of silver in the grass beneath the tree.

"Ah! There you are," she exclaimed as she took two steps forward to retrieve the dagger.

It was only her Elven reflexes that saved Enyri. She grasped the hilt of the dagger and threw herself to the side as the wounded bearak lunged toward her. Quick as she was, the creature's claws caught her upper left thigh leaving a pair of bloody gashes showing through her torn legging.

Ignoring the pain as best she could, the young Elf-ess moved to put as much distance between her and the bearak as possible. She backed up beneath the tree she had just descended from, holding her dagger in a tight grasp, close to her body where it was ready for a deadly thrust.

Hatred and fury burned in the beast's eyes as it lay there gasping for breath, the broken shaft of her arrow still lodged in its throat. The bearak's body was twisted at an odd angle and its lower half appeared useless. Enyri surmised that it had broken its spine when it fell to the ground the night before. Nonetheless the beast was intent on reaching its prey. Its bloodshot eyes followed Enyri's every move as she reached out for the bow and quiver leaning against the tree.

The bearak had felt their sting before and had no intention of doing so again. Digging the claws of its extended paw into the earth, it launched itself forward, swiping at Enyri with the other set of claws.

Enyri danced to the side escaping the attack, but moving away from her bow in the process.

Air and blood were now bubbling from the wound on the bearak's throat with each gasping breath it took. Slowed by its wounds, it seemed no less determined to make a kill and prepared for another lunge.

Enyri timed her dodge as best she could and thrust her dagger into the beast's back as it landed beside her. Pulling the dagger free, she jumped back out of its reach, her wounded leg nearly giving way beneath her.

The bearak gave a strangled roar of pain and anger then worked its way around to face the retreating Elf.

Enyri marveled at the spawn's reserve of strength. Even though it was clearly dying right before her, it still was set on taking its prey with it. Keeping her eyes glued to the beast, she tried to work her way back to her bow. The bearak scooted around, trying its best to remain between her and her goal, but its failing strength slowed its movement a little more with each passing moment. This fact allowed Enyri to work her way through the underbrush and small boulders until she found a safer approach to her weapon. She took her eyes off the bearak for just a moment to gauge the distance to her goal.

From somewhere the creature was able to gain the strength for one more lunge just before she was able to snatch up her bow. It missed the young Elfess with its claws this time, but knocked her down, wrapped a hairy arm around her, and pulled her up against its own body. Its bloody fangs were straining to reach her throat.

Enyri was able to shove the creature's head to the side and bring her dagger to bear, thrusting it deep between the bearak's ribs. Thanks to the dagger's keen edge and greater length, it pierced the spawn's heart, and the bearak died still clasping her to its side.

Fortunately, the huge creature did not land fully on Enyri, and she was able to work her way out of its death grip. After wiping her blade on the bearak's fur, she used the end of her tattered cloak to cleanse the last of the blood from its sharp edge. She hugged the dagger to herself as she breathed a silent thank you to Renthalas for his thoughtful gift. If not for the blade, she would now be as dead as the bearak there before her.

The throbbing in her leg reminded Enyri that she needed to cleanse and treat her wound. She could hear a small stream gurgling over some stones not far from her resting place. Using her leg as little as possible, she pulled herself over to her scattered belongings. Slowly, with just a few twinges of pain, she gathered them up and looked around for something she could use as a staff to help her make her way down to the water's edge.

There in the shrub beside her, Enyri saw a thin branch sticking out toward her. It was straight and appeared sturdy, and from what she could see, it was exactly the right size and length to use for a walking staff. Now all she needed was to find a way to break or cut it loose without further injuring her leg. She reached up and grasped the top of the branch just below a small ring of twigs that crowned it and began pulling it down toward her. To her surprise, it came free in her hand with just that slight tug.

"Thanks to Kyrios!" she breathed as she slowly used the staff to pull herself upright. Carefully she made her way to the nearby stream leaning heavily on her new support. Gingerly, Enyri lowered herself down near the water's edge. She cut a piece of cloth from the hem of her tunic and began cleansing the wound. The claw marks were not as deep as she had feared, but were still extremely painful. The cool water eased the throbbing somewhat. She then bound and treated the wound as best she could with the supplies in her pack. Her task accomplished, she eased back onto her elbow for a brief rest, her wounded leg stretched out before her. Resting there she chewed a piece of dried venison from her stores and let her thoughts calm as she contemplated her next move.

Once again the call that had started this adventure began pulling at her, now more urgent than ever. She turned her gaze up toward the boulders and rocks spilling out into the forest's edge. Somewhere up there was where she needed to go.

"I have a feeling that this is not going to be fun at all," she thought, "but I cannot stay here forever. I might as well try standing up."

She placed the end of the staff firmly on the ground in front of her and used it to pull herself upright. Her leg still pained her, but she realized that even though she would need to move slowly, she would be able to go on without a great deal of suffering.

Slowly and carefully, Enyri made her way out of the 'Wood and into the rocks before her. With the help of the staff, she made much better progress than she had feared would be the case. She was forced to rest much more often than she would have liked, but the exertion did not seem to make her wound pain her more. The climb took many twists and turns through the tumble of stones as she worked her way higher up the slope.

Aware of the dangerous creatures she might find as she moved further from the 'Wood, Enyri kept a sharp eye out for tracks of any kind. For the most part, the ground was hard and rocky, but in sheltered spots where earth had collected, she did find several.

"That's strange," she murmured to herself as she stopped to rest once again, "most of these tracks are moving away from where I seem to be heading."

She took more notice of the tracks as she resumed her climb. Sure enough, more and more the tracks showed creatures leaving the area she was now in instead of entering it.

Forced to rest her wounded leg once more, Enyri leaned against a rock and let her eyes drift up the steep slope ahead. To her surprise, she saw the mouth of a small cave not far above her position. There was a roughly

26

round area before the opening that was several feet in diameter. This area was so clear of plants or stones it was almost as if it had been swept clean.

"It looks like a doorstep," she thought in wonder.

As her gaze rested on the cave, the mental urging grew in strength.

"Guess that is where I am going," she stated, resting her weight on her staff. "I sure hope there are no unwelcoming occupants waiting for me."

Enyri hitched her pack, bow, and quiver to rest more comfortably on her back and started toward the beckoning cave. She let her eyes scan the ground as she moved, looking for the easiest path as the fatigue from her injury and exertion was beginning to grow heavier. She had reached the edge of what she thought of as the doorstep when she came to a surprised halt. There were no tracks on the cleared area at all! Tracks would come up to the edge then circle around it or turn back the way they had come.

"There is something strange at work here," she thought as she studied the ground. She worked her way first around to the north of the doorstep, then to the south, and finally back to her original approach. There was no mistake. Every path of every creature, no matter how big or small, that came upon the cave veered round the cleared area.

"Definitely something strange at work here," she mused with a slight shake of her head.

Enyri roused from her musings when she noticed that the sun was beginning to sink behind the mountain range before her. Soon the light would be gone. If the cave was her destination, now was the time to investigate.

Tentatively, the young Elfess placed her foot on the "doorstep" before her, wondering if she would be turned aside like all the creatures had been. A feeling of peace flowed over her like a gentle rain, but the call or urging became almost a physical entity. Taking a deep breath and grasping her walking staff just a bit more tightly, Enyri made her way to the mouth of the cave. When she reached it, she turned to look behind her. Seeing her lone footprints across the doorstep sent a small shiver up her spine. There was a force at work here that she did not understand. Choosing for the moment not to dwell on what that force might be, she ducked down and entered the cave opening.

Enyri was able to stand to her full height once through the mouth of the cave. She could make out little in the darkness before her. She stepped to the side of the entrance, hoping to let more light through. As she did this, her staff bumped against something lying on the floor of the cave. Bending down to investigate, she found a small torch. How it came to be there did not even cross her mind as she knelt down, as best she could, and used her flint and steel to light it.

With a hiss and a sputter the torch came to life and cast a soft glow around the young Elfess. She raised the light over her head. She was not sure what she had expected to see, but the sight before her was not it. There was nothing there! The rough rock walls of the somewhat circular room arched up to form a domed ceiling, just feet above her head. The walls, floor, and ceiling appeared to be native rock. It was the type of cave she had seen many times in the past. Usually, a cave like this would have contained the remains of an animal's bed, and quite possibly its last meal.

This small empty room? This was what she had worked so hard to reach?

Enyri gave a sigh along with a shake of her head. There was no logic here. No reason she could see that she should have felt drawn to this place.

"When I saw this cave, I just knew something important was here," she murmured. "But there is nothing. Nothing but an empty call in my mind."

Sadly, she turned, preparing to leave the cave, but came up short as she reached the door. There was nothing there to stop her. There was no reason why she could not just walk out of the cave and limp her way back to Iniriand and her father's halls. For some reason, she felt almost as if there was a hand against her chest, an arm barring her exit.

"This is foolish!" she turned and once more scanned the wall around her. "Why should I stay here? What is so important?"

Suddenly there was a sharp *crack,* and a slab of rock broke free from just off center in the back wall, exposing a deep niche it had been hiding.

"All right, so that is why I should stay."

Enyri hobbled to the back of the room to investigate. The niche was just above her eye level, but as she stretched up as far as her wounded leg would allow, she could see that there was something hidden away inside. Making use of a deep crack left by the falling rock, she firmly wedged the base of the torch in place, freeing her hands. The Elfess reached up into the small opening to retrieve the object that was hidden there. Her hand came in contact with something that felt like a smooth, wooden box, and she gently lifted it out of its resting place. As she lowered this object down to where she could grasp it with both hands, the call that she had been following, the feeling of urgency that had drawn her here, ended. The physical release was so great it made her catch her breath in surprise, and caused her to gaze at the object she held in wonder.

Enyri eased her way down to rest on the floor, since there was nothing in the cave to sit on. She sat with her back against the wall under the torch where its light would be to the best advantage. Giving a small wince, she stretched her wounded leg out in front of her and laid her staff across her lap. Slowly, she turned her find around in her hands, examining every inch of it. It appeared to be a single piece of wood, not a box. There was no seam or crack, no latch or hinge, just a solid block without mark or adornment, polished to a wonderful smoothness, and covered in a fine layer of dust.

"This is what called me here?"

She lightly brushed at the dust, then, with a gentle breath, she blew to remove the last clinging remnants.

Before she could again inhale, something began to happen to the block. It grew warm in her hands and began to glow softly. Soon that glow began to grow brighter and brighter until Enyri was forced to turn her head to shield her eyes. With a loud pop, the block split in two, the top portion lifting to reveal a small compartment.

Speechless, Enyri simply gaped at the box she held for a moment before thinking to see what was hidden inside. There, nestled in velvet, was a dull, dark green stone, approximately the size of her clenched fist, only longer. The stone had not been cut or polished, yet it was extremely smooth with no sharp edges as she ran her finger over its bumpy surface. Being one to enjoy the tactile qualities of objects, a small smile raised the corners of her mouth, and her eyes grew bright with delight as she cupped the stone in her hands.

The stone began to throb and pulse with light. This took Enyri so by surprise that she gave a start, causing her to lose her grip on it. Fearing the stone would fall to the floor and shatter, the Elfess tried to catch it in the air. The stone seemed to jump away from her hand and toward the head of her walking staff. The crown of twigs came alive, caught the stone, grew up and twined about it. As the two items joined, there was a burst of emerald green light that shot out and struck Enyri's wounded leg.

The Elfess gave a small cry of surprise and dropped the staff to the floor as she grabbed for her leg. To her amazement, she realized the pain of her wound was gone. Quickly she pulled Renthalas' dagger from her boot and cut the cords holding her bandage in place. Showing through the bloody hole in her leggings was her wounded thigh, pink and smooth and perfectly healed. There was not a mark on it.

Tentatively, she reached for the staff and lifted it from the rocky floor. The heart of the stone took on a soft glow at her touch, and she stared at it in amazement. Her confusion quickly gave way to her curiosity. She placed the staff across her lap once more and retrieved the box to examine it more closely. Beneath the place where the stone had rested, she found a thin sheet of fine, folded parchment. Feeling that her questions would soon be answered, at least in part, she gently smoothed it out flat and raised it to the light of the torch so she could read the script she found written on it:

"Greetings to you, my young student,

If you are reading this missive it means that you have been chosen as my apprentice. During my meditations, I was directed by Kyrios to place both the stone and staff you now possess in their separate hiding places. If you have felt the call and have found this note, it means that Kyrios has chosen you for a great calling. The calling of becoming one of His wizards and doing your part to combat the forces of evil that nearly surround us.

Obtaining your staff is the first step on your journey. The path to becoming a full wizard in the service of Kyrios is long and arduous. It will lead not to fame or fortune, but to blessings beyond compare.

For your calling, you must first and foremost learn patience. Return to your home, and in due time I will be drawn to you.

Until we meet, study and meditate on all that has happened.

A"

Enyri slowly read the letter once more before lowering it, her hand coming to rest on the wooden box in her lap. She sat there for several moments, her eyes fixed on the items she held, but not really seeing them.

"A wizard's apprentice," she breathed in wonder. "Who could have guessed this was what my thirst to learn and understand would have led to?" Her amazement was magnified by the fact that of the known wizards, only one was an Elf. All others came from the race of Man.

Still pondering the wonder of her situation, Enyri carefully refolded the parchment and returned it to the box, then placed both inside her pack. Night had fallen, and she prepared to rest right where she was before beginning her journey back through the Tharonwood to her father's halls in Iniriand the next morning.

Her last thoughts as she drifted off to sleep brought a smile to her face. "It is good that it was me and not Alynniel who was chosen for this path. Patience is *not* one of my sister's many virtues."

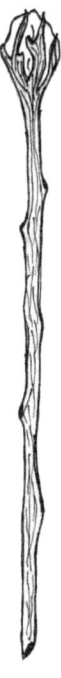

The Madgician and the Vorpal Sword

C. K. Deatherage

L uwys, firstborn son of the House of Khaerel, tightened his grip on Vorpal. The sword vibrated slightly in his hand, signaling the presence of his quarry nearby. Silver-gold light flickered along the gleaming edges of the blade. Vorpal was ready—Luwys only hoped he could match the sword's fervor when the beast attacked. For he had no doubt the creature would; it could sense Vorpal's presence as readily as the sword sensed the creature's.

Luwys tensed and crouched as several Borogoves fluttered nervously into the air, their normally forlorn calls turning to shrieks of alarm. He studied the direction they flew—off to his left. Better focus his attention to the right, then. The heavy foliage of the large-leaved TümTüm trees cast dark shadows on the tulgey undergrowth beneath.

A flock of Karkamews darted nearly straight up, then flew high over his head. The beast was closing in, he was sure. Vorpal's eagerness intensified, its light becoming a steady beam, energy pulsating through his hand and into his arm. His own anticipation increased, and he forced himself to breathe slowly. His heart rate calmed, his focus sharpening as the sound of clawed feet crunched the fallen twigs to his right. Vorpal rang with power.

Dark yellow eyes rose nearly to the level of the lowest branches, still many feet high, of the nearest Tüm-Tüm trees. Their black, dragon-like slits narrowed, focusing on Luwys. The young warrior-knight knew better than to gaze into those amber orbs, but since he'd been spotted, there was no point in taking a defensive posture. He stood, feet spread in a wide, stable stance, Vorpal clutched firmly in a two-handed grip.

Luwys heard the beast's angry snarl. He felt his own lips curl in response. "So," he said, "you recognize my companion." He swung Vorpal in a tight circle. The creature rumbled deep in its chest. Luwys smiled grimly. "Yes, you know Vorpal. My great-great-grandfather slew the Jabberwock with it, and my grandfather ended the life of the Jubjub. You are the last of the Manxome Foe to plague fair Vündorlönde." He paused and shook his head. "You should never have returned from the banishment placed upon you by the White Queen. For now . . . you must die!"

The rumble emanating from the shadowed creature grew deeper. Luwys braced himself for the coming attack.

"Banisshment issn't all it'ss meant to be." The beast emerged from the forest's shadows, its red-gold scales glistening in the light of the brillig sun. Long black claws sunk their curved points into a moss-covered log, sending tiny Sqweelishees flittering into the woods. Again the deep rumbling burst forth from the creature's throat, as it raised its horned head and gaped wide its many-fanged maw before snapping it shut.

With a surge of horror, Luwys realized the beast was laughing. Momentarily taken off guard, he raised his eyes to the creature's face. Immediately, the monster pinned him with its slitted gaze. Too late, Luwys remembered to avoid the creature's stare. He felt his limbs grow numb, and he could barely sense Vorpal's thrumming hilt in his stiff fingers. This was the *mesmerspel* his grandfather had warned him about. He fought to look away, but those amber orbs drew him further in, draining away his strength and resolve. Vorpal raged in vain, silver-gold light sparking dangerously, as the blade slowly dipped to the ground. *Fool!* Luwys berated himself. *You fool! You are the last of the monster-hunters, and if you fail, the Bandersnatch will rend your worthless hide and ravage Vündorlönde once more. And father will have died in vain. Move, Luwys! Just look away. . . .*

The Bandersnatch lowered its bulk until its horned head was but a few feet away from Luwys' face. Luwys could feel its hot breath and smell a certain sweet-rancid odor emanating from the creature's mouth. Still paralyzed, the warrior-knight prepared himself to feel those gleaming fangs, and he was startled when the Bandersnatch spoke once more.

"It'sss too bad I have already eaten—a tasste of manflessh is always a refresshing change. And yourss sssmellss sstrangely familiar. Sstill, I can't have you galumphing through the woodss with that fearceling weapon. Nassty thing, it iss. Much too pain-pointy and ssnicker-ssnacky!" It licked its lips with a black tongue, green drool dripping from its teeth. "I sshall just have to ssacrifice my indigesstion and devour you anyway."

As the Bandersnatch leaned forward, maw agape, Vorpal gave a sudden ring, its light blazing, though its point still rested on the ground. It was enough, however, to cause the beast to glance down at the weapon. The moment the eye contact was broken, Luwys sprang forward, raising Vorpal and thrusting the thrumming weapon into the closest amber-filled socket.

The Bandersnatch roared, rearing backwards, clawing at its face. Again, Luwys struck, the gleaming blade plunging deep into the creature's chest. Black blood spurted forth, splattering Luwys' green hunter's cloak. The Bandersnatch crashed to its side, bending bushrakes beneath its weight. It whurzled deep in its throat. Luwys paused, trying to discern the beast's slurred speech. His brow furrowed with the effort. The sounds emanating from the Bandersnatch made little sense:

> *Destination in dimension*
> *Planet in the Sun's suspension,*
> *I this mortal forth do cast,*
> *For the death of Bandersnatch . . .*

The last of the Manxome Foe burbled its final breath, the red-gold gleam of is scales growing dull, its dark dragonish eye-slits gazing blankly at the brillig sky. Luwys felt a twinge of regret, though he knew there had been no choice in the slaying of the creature. It had already eaten all the cattlekine near at hand and had sampled several flocks of bahwuls on the slopes of Greinlee. And once the livestock were gone, the villagers would have been next. And there was the revenge-factor. The Bandersnatch had killed his father before being banished by the White Queen's Madgician. Still . . . Luwys shook his head, sheathing his sword, and turned to leave.

He had taken but two steps, when the woods seemed to implode, the ground rising to swallow him, the giant TümTüm trees bending down to engulf him in their voluminous branches. The mournful coo of the Borogoves mixed with the roar of the wind as the last words of the Bandersnatch replayed upon the currents:

Destination in dimension . . .

Luwys felt as if his body were being simultaneously crunched and stretched. Colors mixed and blurred together. He could barely breathe and what air he could draw in held a sweet-rancid odor. Then everything went black. He wondered if he had indeed had the life crushed from him, except the beast's words kept echoing into the darkness.

Planet in the Sun's suspension . . .

Suddenly, lights flickered before his eyes, streaks of white and blue and red and yellow, the yellow growing the brightest until it filled all his vision. Then, the lights slowed and coalesced into tiny pin-pricks. He gasped. He was among the stars! A large yellow-orange ball of flame receded into the distance behind him as he hurtled towards a small blue-green sphere.

I this mortal forth do cast . . .

Luwys felt as if a huge fist had flung him forward. The blue-green sphere grew larger until it was all he could see. His skin, if indeed, he still wore a body, felt hot as he plunged downward into the sphere. Suddenly, all color vanished into a gray mist, and his body cooled and slowed as if he were floating in a cloud. Perhaps he was. Then, the gray faded and there was nothing, not even darkness. Just nothing. Nothing except the words:

For the death of Bandersnatch!

Is this death? he wondered until even his wondering ceased.

* * * *

"Hey, man."

Luwys groaned. He felt someone shaking him by his left shoulder, but his body refused to move. Even his eyelids felt weighted down.

"You don't look so hot. They got a good meal going down at the shelter. Come on, man. Wake up."

More shoulder-shaking. At last Luwys felt his eyelids lift, however sluggishly. His eyes fastened on the dark-skinned youth hovering over him. He blinked in the light of a teatime sun. "Where . . . am I?" His voice sounded as raspy as a Scritchdaw.

The youth grinned. "That's better, man. You had me worried. You're in the alley near 12th and Main. You must've had a wild night last night. My dad can help. He's the preacher at the shelter."

Luwys blinked. The youth obviously spoke a foreign dialect as half of the words he couldn't understand. "I . . . my name is Luwys, son of Lord Khaerel," he offered, hoping his young rescuer could comprehend his speech. He struggled to rise to his feet, grateful for the youth's assistance. The world seemed to swirl a moment, then steady out. He let his gaze travel down the narrow alleyway, then up along the buildings to either side, and he nearly collapsed again. He had shrunk! It was as if he had eaten from the Great Caterpillar's mushroom and reduced in size to a cat! The buildings, mostly made from a dingy brown brick, towered over him—windows, barred and locked, peppering the sides with black metal ladders zig-zagging their way down to the gravel below.

With pounding heart, he grabbed the youth's arm, demanding, "What did you do to me? Make me big again."

"Whoa, man." The boy pulled out a small metal vial. "Unless you want a snootful of pepper spray, let go of the arm."

Again, the youth's words were more mystery than sense, but Luwys understood the last part. He released his grip, but remained on guard. "I seek your pardon, but I am at a loss to explain my circumstances."

"Yeah, well, whatever you took last night, don't take it again. It'll rot your brain, for sure." The youth studied him a moment, then shook his head, stuffing the metal vial back into his pants pocket. "You're one of those MagnifiCon USA people, aren't you? The cloak and sword thing is cool, but you must've slept in a garbage bin last night 'cause whatever you got all over your clothes stinks like a dead dog."

Luwys sniffed. He did stink. He looked down at his clothes and realized they were spattered with the dark, dried blood of the Bandersnatch. "I need to wash," he admitted. "Is there a stream nearby?"

His companion just shook his head. "Drop the MagnifiCon act, will ya? We got showers and a laundromat at the shelter. Come on."

Not knowing what else to do, Luwys followed. As they emerged from the alley, Luwys hung back, his hand trembling on the hilt of his sword. Tall buildings ran the length of the broad roadway, which was hard and paved with a strange gray-black substance. But it was the beasts that galumphed along the path that most startled him. Shiny and multi-colored, they roared past him on round legs, some squonking like a Downybird, all seeming to race pell-mell to some unknown destination. One beast darted to the side of the road and stopped. To his horror, its mouth opened and disgorged a woman!

"What is this place?" he murmured, heart pounding fearfully. With the rushing and squonking of the shiny beasts, the youth appeared not to hear him; he continued to walk down the path bordering the roadway as if no danger were nearby. Taking a deep breath, Luwys followed, though his hand remained firmly on Vorpal's hilt in case any of those man-devouring beasts took an interest in him or his companion.

After walking several blocks, turning left twice and right once, they paused before a low brick building with a hand-painted sign over the doorway, which read *Haven's Rest* in bright gold letters edged in black. The young man grinned. "Welcome to the shelter! We arrived just in time for dinner. Come on."

Luwys felt his mouth watering at the aroma that met him upon entering the building. Long tables with an assortment of chairs filled the large room, while a long line of people, mostly older, rather bedraggled-looking men, filed past a counter against the far wall where two younger men and three women piled food onto the trays the people in the line were holding. Luwys felt his young companion tug his arm.

"Go on, get in line. I need to help serve the food. Trays are over there. Pick up a plate and silverware. Water and lemonade are in the coolers to the left."

Luwys grasped his arm, though lightly, lest the youth pull out his magic vial of *pepper spray* again. "I do not know your name. How may I address you?"

The dark-skinned youth grinned. "I'm Ray. My Dad's name is Franklin, though everyone just calls him *Preacher*. Gotta go. See ya in a few, Lou!"

Luwys raised his hand in the same gesture Ray gave as the young man darted away. "See *ya*, Ray, son of Franklin, Preacher of Haven's Rest," he said quietly. He wondered if a Preacher were akin to a Manor Lord and if the straggling line of feasters were the Preacher's serfs. If so, they were well-fed—though he wondered where the fields were that the serfs would have labored in.

Watching the men around him, Luwys placed the plate and eatingware on his tray and walked to the feeding booth. There one lady plopped a large helping of something white and fluffy on his plate, the next lady placed brown liquid on the fluff, and the last, a hefty, cheerful-looking man, put a large serving of roast beef with carrots beside the drenched fluff. The aroma almost covered up the stench of Bandersnatch blood on his clothing. Adding a cup of some yellow liquid to his tray, Luwys sat down at a table next to a gray-haired, bent old man who smelled of sweat and other undefinables. Luwys was fascinated by the man's gray handle-bar mustache. It made him look much like a very crotchety old walrus he knew.

"Name's Richard," the old man said, shoveling in a mouthful of carrots. "Never seen you b'fore. Wass your name?"

"Luwys, son of Khaerel." Luwys found himself forking his food into his mouth quickly—both because he realized he was famished and because that seemed to be the preferred method of eating at Haven's Rest.

"Well, Lewis," Richard said, eyeing Luwys' plate, "you might not want to eat the taters—instant stuff, not the real thing. Gives you gas—unless you're used to them. Like me. If you don't want them, I'll finish 'em up for you. The folks that run the place won't know the difference. Makes 'em feel good if all the plates come back empty."

Luwys had already eaten part of the brown-covered fluff—and it tasted delicious. But he slid his plate over for Richard to finish the *taters*. He didn't want *gas*—whatever that was, and Richard looked like he could probably use a little extra food.

The old man sat back, a contented smile showing beneath his mustache. He gave a drawn out belch, then said, "Time for the preachin'. Best sit back and enjoy yourself . . . What *is* that smell?" He sniffed under his own arm, then shrugged. Without the aroma of the dinner wafting in the air, the Bandersnatch blood on Luwys' clothes began to permeate the immediate atmosphere. Luwys stood up.

"Perhaps I'd best wash myself and my garments," he said. "I do not wish to give offense."

Richard laughed. "Sit down, boy! Ain't no one

bathing or doing their clothes till after the preachin'. Them's the rules."

Luwys sat down, the man on the other side of him edging away a little and making a face. He watched as a dark-skinned man stepped out of the crowd of tables and mounted a small platform. *That must be Preacher, Ray's father,* he thought. He noticed the crowd went immediately silent, every eye trained on the man up front. Then the Preacher began to speak. Many of the words Luwys could not understand, but one thing stood out to him: the Preacher wanted him to seek the truth—and there was a lot of truth he needed to know, like where he was and how he got here and how to get back. After the Preacher stepped down, Luwys turned to Richard and asked, "Is this place part of Vünderlönde, perhaps the northeastern portion? I've never been there before."

Richard laughed, a hoarse, gravelly sound. "Ain't no Wonderland around here—unless you mean that MagnifiCon USA thingy. This here is downtown Chicago, mister. Where you from, anyways?"

She-Kahgoh? Luwys felt his stomach drop. He wondered for a moment if he would experience *gas,* but the feeling quickly passed. He'd never heard of *She-Kahgoh.* A cold chill swept over him. The Bandersnatch had sent him to a World Beyond! It would take a great Madgician to return him to his land, someone powerful enough to untwordle the beast's curse.

His mind raced. Both Richard and Ray Preacherson had mentioned MagnifiCon USA. Perhaps that would be a place to start. The name itself fairly oogled of magic.

"Hey, Lou!"

Luwys turned in the direction of the voice. He smiled

as Ray hurried toward him. As the young man drew near, Ray scrunched up his face and blew through his lips. "Eew, man! You stink worse now than when I first found you. Let's get you cleaned up and find your bunk." Luwys followed his friend closely, winding his way through tables and lounging men until he entered a room marked *showers*.

"There's soap and shampoo in each stall," Ray was saying. "Draw the curtain and toss me your clothes. I'll go get them washed. There's some sweats on the bench in the shower you can borrow till tomorrow."

Feeling a bit awkward, Luwys stripped off his trousers, shirt, tunic and cloak, but he kept his belt, sword, and scabbard, setting them on the bench next to the gray clothing. He threw his wadded up garments over the curtain, eliciting a disgusted exclamation from Ray. Then he stared at the metal fixtures before him. There was a bar that appeared to turn. He turned it a little and cold water hit him in the face. Desperately, he grasped the bar to try to turn off the spray, but pulled it the wrong way. The water turned hot. "Yeeoww!" he yelled and quickly adjusted the handle to the middle. At last he could enjoy the warm waterfall that sprayed from the nozzle above. Definitely, this land had magic. The waterfall was plainly a special enchantment in itself. He poured a sweet-smelling liquid into his hands from a bottle sitting on a small shelf and scrubbed himself clean of Bandersnatch gore. The soap he used at home was made of lye and felt rough, but this soap seemed most bewitching in its smooth texture and aroma. He certainly felt better after washing with it.

Slipping on the soft gray sweats, Luwys pulled back the curtain and stepped out of the enchanted water room. Ray was waiting for him.

"Man! I nearly chucked your clothes, Lou. But I know costumes cost a pretty penny, so I persuaded Sandra to wash them. You can thank me later."

Luwys didn't know why he had to wait to thank his new friend, but he nodded and followed Ray to a room with two rows of bunk beds. "This one's yours. Bunk 17." Ray patted a top bunk two-thirds of the way down the room and to the right. "I see you kept your props. Keep them with you at all times. We can't guarantee against theft, I'm afraid."

Luwys assumed Ray meant his sword and belt when he said *props,* so he strapped them on immediately. The sweats were a little big, and the belt helped hold them in place. "Ray Preacherson," he began, "can you take me to MagnifiCon USA tomorrow? I must find a Madgician who can help me get home."

Ray looked at him skeptically. "You mean old Hatfield the Magnificent? I hear he's playing at MagnifiCon." Ray sighed, then shrugged. "Well. I got the day off tomorrow, and I've saved up some cash, so I guess I can get us into MagnifiCon USA. It's not really my thing—all those geeks in costumes, pretending they're somebody they aren't. Still, it's been a long time since I've seen Hatfield. Used to be one of our customers till he finally got his act together—literally." He grinned, then nodded. "It's a deal. But you got to promise me no more drugs or sleeping in alleys."

Luwys blinked. He wasn't sure what Ray meant but since he didn't think he had any *drugs* and was positive he never again wanted to sleep in dark corners between tall buildings, it was easy to agree. "I promise, Ray Preacherson. And thank you."

The next morning, after a breakfast that Luwys actually recognized—hotcakes, sausage, and eggs—Ray handed him his freshly laundered garments, which he quickly put on. The gray sweats had been quite comfortable but had left Luwys feeling a little underclothed.

"Thank you, Ray Preacherson," he said as he fastened his green hunter's cloak about his neck. "And thank Sandra for washing my clothing."

"Yeah," Ray chuckled, "I had to trade a week's worth of dishwashing to get her to do it. You owe me, man!" He punched Luwys in the arm in a friendly fashion.

Luwys frowned. "I'm afraid I have no coinage with me, Ray Preacherson. But perhaps I could render you some sort of service instead."

Ray snorted. "You could render me a great service by dropping the *Preacherson* thing. I'm just Ray."

"Very well, . . . Ray." Luwys felt he was doing his friend a disservice by leaving off his title, but if that's what he desired—so be it.

Ray then led him out the door of Haven's Rest, down the street, and to a covered bench, where one lone woman sat, balancing a large bag in her lap. "We'll wait here for the bus," Ray said. They didn't wait long before a huge silver beast came galumphing up, pausing with a loud screech beside the bench. Luwys placed one hand on Vorpal's hilt as the beast threw wide its maw—revealing three steps. With a grunt, the woman hoisted herself and her bag up the steps and into the belly of the beast. Ray followed. Letting go of his sword, but with thlunking heart, Luwys followed. Strangely, there were booth seats inside the creature and glass-covered holes in the beast's side. Sitting down, Luwys watched, fascinated, as the creature sped up and roared along. So many tall buildings! So many gwonking beasts on the road! So many absurdly-dressed people on the sidewalks!

As they drew near a large building, Luwys saw more people dressed normally, like himself, mixed with those who dressed oddly, like Ray, mixed with strange creatures in even stranger garments—or lack thereof. One female seemed to have green skin—mostly bare—with delicate fish-netting and flowers placed just barely over the necessities. The White Queen would have taken the poor girl, counseled her, and given her fresh white gowns to wear. The Red Queen would have had her head long ago just for the impropriety of it all!

The bus pulled alongside a covered area—no bench this time—and cranked open its mouth again. Luwys felt relieved to be out in the open as the long, lanky creature roared off. Heading inside the building, Luwys followed his friend to a rather long line of variously attired people. At least most appeared to be human. Some Luwys wasn't so sure. One creature had bushy dark hair, horns, and tusks protruding from the corners of its mouth—which tended to make it drool. The language it used while waiting impatiently in line made Luwys surmise the creature was related to the infamous Cockamuth. Their verbiage was reported to make even the Red Queen blush.

At last they reached the booth where Ray paid for two badges which were worn on a string round the neck. The man at the booth eyed Vorpal sheathed at Luwys' side. "You gotta peace-bind that if you want in. No loose weaponry," he said. He held up a thin leather strip. "Five bucks."

Ray snorted. "Five dollars for a piece of boot string?"

The man shrugged. "Five dollars or you don't get in with that sword."

Grumbling, under his breath, Ray plunked down his money and grabbed the string, handing it to Luwys. "Here, bind the thing."

Luwys obligingly wrapped the leather strip around the hilt and tied it to his belt. He fervently hoped he'd not have need to draw Vorpal quickly—and he threw a cautious glance at the foul-mouthed Cockamuth-like thing. It was sauntering through two large doors opened wide with guards posted on either side. One guard checked the tag the creature was wearing and waved it on in.

As they walked away from the booth, Ray did his friendly punch on Luwys' arm again. He leaned in and spoke lowly, "Last night, my dad made a call to a friend who made a call to a friend, and he got us backstage passes to see Hatfield the Magnificent! I kinda look forward to seeing the old guy. It's nice to see 'em when they're sobered up and doing well, ya know?"

Luwys didn't comprehend most of what Ray whispered, but he took it as good news. "So we will see the Madgician?" he asked.

"Yeah, man. That's what I'm saying. We're going backstage right now. He's got a show later, if you want to see it."

Ray led him to a side door with its own special guard who scanned their passes carefully, nodded, then opened the door, waving them through. "Third door on the right," he said brusquely.

Upon reaching the door, Ray winked at Luwys and whispered. "Hatfield is a bit eccentric, you know? Has this fetish about hats. Wears a different one for different occasions." Then he gave three sharp raps.

"Who's there?" came a rather cautious, older male voice.

"It's me, Mr. Hatfield—Raymond from Haven's Rest. I was hoping to visit a bit before your show. We heard you're a real hit at the Cons and in Vegas. Dad's real proud of you."

The knob rattled and slowly the door creaked open. A white-bearded man with wild white hair, barely covered by a tan pith helmet, and equally wild eyebrows peeked out. He broke into a wide grin, throwing open the door and motioning for them to come in. "It *is* you, Ray, my boy! Can't be too careful nowadays, you know. And who's your friend?"

"This here is Lou. He really wanted to meet you. Apparently, he's keen on magic and magicians."

As Luwys stepped forward to greet his host, he felt a sudden vibration at his left side. Vorpal was thrumming! A bit of light shown where the hilt met the scabbard. He gazed hard at the Madgician, wondering if Vorpal were responding to good—or evil—power.

"Ah!" Hatfield the Magnificent seemed both surprised and extraordinarily pleased as his deep blue eyes glittered appreciatively, fixed on Luwys' sword. He glanced at Ray, who seemed unaware of what Vorpal was doing.

Just then, Ray's cellphone chirped. He punched it on. "Yeah? Ray here." He listened a moment; then his face fell. "Yeah. All right. I'll be there in a few." He thrust his phone deep into his pocket and gave a disgusted snort. "What do you know but Chuck's sick again. I gotta go cover for him, but I can be back in time for the show in a few hours. If we don't meet up at the show, Lou, wait for me near the badge booth afterwards, okay?"

"I will try, Ray," Luwys answered honestly. He *thought* he remembered where the badge booth was. He watched and waved as Ray dashed out the door. Then he turned to the old man and eyed him cautiously. "So," he patted his vibrating scabbard, "Vorpal tells me you are a true Madgician. Do you serve the White Queen or the Red?"

The man gave a low chuckle. "Brave young hero to face a powerful Madgician with a peace-bound sword! Fortunately for you, I actually know what you're talking about. I serve the White Queen."

He motioned for Luwys to take a seat. "Let me fix us a bit of tea, while I tell you my tale." He removed his pith helmet and studied his collection of hats, deciding on a green crushed velvet top hat. "This is my favorite for teatime," he said with a wink. "Such a classic!" he added as he walked over to the sink and filled a teapot with water, setting it on a portable electric hotplate. As the water began to murmur, heating up, Hatfield sat down across from Luwys.

"Back in Vündorlönde, I was known as THE Hatter, the most powerful Madgician among Her Majesty's mages. So it was, when the great monster-hunter, your father, was slain by the Bandersnatch, the Queen asked me to banish the monster using magic. This I did, but there was one catch—the magic that banished the creature also banished *me* to a realm with very little magic. And without magic, I could not return. So, here I have been for years upon years. It truly drove me mad at one point—but, thankfully, young Raymond and his father, the Preacher, helped me to get back on my feet. I studied the arts and sleight of hand of this world's so-called magicians, and found I was quite good at the simple trickeries they call *magic*. And so, I became Hatfield the Magnificent."

Hatfield stood up and fetched the tea kettle, a teapot, and two cups. Setting them down on a rickety side table, he carefully poured the hot water into the pot and placed a shiny silver teaball inside. He replaced the cracked lid and sat back down. "But now you bring a powerful weapon just oogling with magic! With it I should be able to get us both home. That is, if I can remember the right enchantment." He began muttering something as he poured the dark tea into the cups and handed one to Luwys.

"Thank you, honored Madgician," the young warrior said. He swallowed a sip, then leaned forward eagerly. "Did you know my father, sir? He died when I was quite young, only a weebling, really. I vaguely remember a tall man with black hair and dark brown eyes and a wonkling laugh, but I'm not sure of the memory."

Hatfield gave a chuckle. "Oh, that was him, all right! Tall and winselm and with a perkly smile that had all the ladies twittlepated. And a mighty warrior too." He shook his head. "What an unksum day when he was . . . yes, well . . . *taken*."

Luwys sipped his tea without saying a word. He really didn't remember his father very well, but his mother had told him the stories of his bravery and kindness. He hoped to live up to his father's reputation. And he'd made a good start by killing the beast that had killed his father and saving Vündorlönde from its depredations. He cleared his throat.

"So, sir, should I remain with you to have Vorpal at hand when you remember the right enchantment?" He worried a little what Ray would think about his sudden allegiance to the old Madgician. He sometimes felt the young man thought he was a trifle mad himself.

"That won't be a problem my beamish young hero. Just let me attire myself aright, and the enchantment is mine." Gulmping down the last of his tea, Hatfield moved to his collection of chapeaus, removing the top hat and replacing it with a puffy purple tam adorned with a red fuzzball on top. "Nothing like a tam to aid memory. Let's see now...." The old man was silent for a few moments, his finger laid beside his nose, tapping. "Ah! I have it! All we need is to both be touching Vorpal when I say the words and whiffle-puff! we're in Vündorlönde just in time for high tea with the White Queen."

Luwys' heart sped up and he clutched Vorpal's buzzing hilt with tense excitement. "Shall we go now, sir?"

Hatfield chortled. "No, no, my impatient hunter! These things must be done properly and in the appropriate setting. What if we just disappeared now? The authorities would think our young friend Raymond had something to do with it as he would have been the last to see us. We don't want to get him in trouble now, do we?"

Luwys swallowed, embarrassed by his anxiousness to leave. Of course, he would not wish ill on Ray, his rescuer, yet he could not keep himself from asking, "When, then, sir?"

The old Madgician leaned forward, a twinkle in one eye. "Ah, tonight, during my show, I will ask you to come forward to assist me. As you do, unbind Vorpal and hand it to me when I say so. Then just follow my instructions. We'll give the audience a taste of real magic, my boy!" He chuckled. "Oh yes, these poor folk, so busy with their cell phones and pads and just busyfulnessishness, will at last see something real. And maybe—just maybe—they will stop their galumphing through life just long enough to consider seeking other truth they may have been missing."

Luwys nodded, thinking back upon the words Preacher had said. If delaying their return home would help others seek truth and keep Ray safe from the authorities, then it was worth waiting—even though the thought of giving up Vorpal temporarily was painful. He stood. "I will do as you say, honorable Madgician."

Hatfield winked. "Doing what your eldsters say is often the better part of wisdom. Then again, I am *mad*, you know. All Madgicians are to some degree. But mad or wise, I'm your only way home, my fine boy. So, let's get to it. Go blend yourself amongst the crowd and head for Stage Three. Move to the front and stay put. I shall be there within the hour. Hatfield the Magnificent's last performance!—at least in this worlds-realm."

* * * *

Fifty-two minutes later, Luwys found himself standing in front of Stage Three, somewhat squished, between the Cockamuth look-alike and the almost naked green woman. Surrounding him were assorted people and two-legged beasts. Some carried strange weapons. Others carried backpacks or colorful bags full of various trinkets, books, cards, posters, games, jewelry, artwork, and in some cases—lunch. Some had human faces. Others were painted with strange designs, while still others wore hoods and masks. Some looked like monsters. Others were pirates or assassins or gypsies or princesses or wizards or warriors or indescribables. Luwys desperately wanted to unbind Vorpal—just in case—but he stoically kept his blade peace-bound as the man at the badge counter had instructed. He noticed many of the pirates and assassins and warriors did the same. MagnifiCon USA must be a place of neutral ground, he reasoned. He looked at the thronging mass behind him, carefully avoiding glancing at the green woman, and tried to spy Ray Preacherson, but if Ray were there, he was indiscernible from the crowd.

Suddenly, a voice announced out of nowhere, echoing in the massive, crowded chamber: "Hatfield the Magnificent, magician extraordinaire, will be performing at Stage Three in five minutes. You don't want to miss the astounding feats of prestidigitation as this master of the mystic arts amazes you with his out-of-this-world production. Come see Hatfield the Magnificent!" Luwys wondered at the voice. It seemed magical in itself, but the Madgician had said there was little magic in this world. He shook his head. So much about this worlds-realm was strange and difficult to understand.

He did not have much time to ponder when with a flash of purple smoke and silver glitter, Hatfield appeared on stage amidst applause. He was dressed more normally in a purple tea jacket with tails, green and black striped trousers, yellow vest, and a simply enormous top hat of bright orange, complete with a blood-red feather. Suitable attire for a Madgician of the White Queen's court. With his wild white hair askew, the Madgician began his performance with giant card tricks, floating ball illusions, flowers that appeared in place of a wand, disappearing doves, and a rabbit appearing out of his coat tails. Luwys was not impressed. None of it was real. He could not imagine why the crowd oohed and aahed at the spectacle. He felt his hands clench and his throat go tight. What if Hatfield were no true Madgician? Should he give up his sword into the hands of a fraud?

"And now, for the grand finale, my greatest feat of magic!" Hatfield intoned in a truly magnificent voice. He pulled out a table, rolling it on wheels. A red cloth, painted with glitter and bright yellow swirls, hung down from the table, obscuring what might lie beneath. Luwys, again, was not impressed. Anyone could see how fake it was. "For this last act," the Madgician continued, voice rising, "I will use—not a trained professional assistant, but one of you!—someone from the audience!"

The crowd bellowed with pleasure and a multitude of hands, paws, claws, and robotic-looking arms rose into the air. Luwys obediently raised his hand with the others, assuming that's what Hatfield would want. The Madgician pretended to scan the crowd intently, while loudly muttering, "The aura must be right... dangerous...I hope my insurance is paid up..." and other such absurdities that only served to whip up the audience into greater enthusiasm. Finally, the Madgician's eyes locked with Luwys' and he nodded sagely, motioning for Luwys to ascend the stage. "I've found the one!" he bellowed as Luwys mounted the three steps and walked across the stage. "That is, if you are brave enough, sir—or mad enough—to entrust your life to Hatfield the Magnificent!"

The crowd clapped. Luwys gave a lopsided grin at the enthusiastic mass of bodies, then turned and bowed to the Madgician. "My life and destiny are in your hands, sir," he said.

"If that is so, give me your sword, young warrior, and I will take plain steel and make it pure magic!" Hatfield's blue eyes bored into his as the old man nodded slightly, holding out his hands.

With a slight sigh, Luwys untied Vorpal and drew it from its scabbard. Immediately, the blade, thrumming from close proximity to the Madgician, burst into brilliant light as he placed it in Hatfield's hands. The crowd roared and clapped. Luwys blinked in the light, his hope returning—perhaps there was real magic left in the Madgician after all.

"And now, my brave assistant, I will not place you inside a box where no one can see you. No, I ask you to lie on this table in plain view of all. No covers, no sheets. Nothing between you and this glowing blade!"

Luwys nodded and carefully climbed onto the table, lying flat on his back. The light from Vorpal was almost too much to bear as Hatfield held it hovering over him. The Madgician began to move the blade in flat circles over Luwys' body.

"And now...for the incantation." Hatfield closed his eyes and intoned:

Destination now suspended
'Snatch's spell forever ended
Vündorlönde and Queen to find
Leave this world and sun behind

Squinting against the blaze of Vorpal's light, Luwys watched as Hatfield raised the sword high and brought it slicing down through the static-filled air toward his middle. Only at the last minute did the Madgician deftly twist the hilt so that the flat of the blade struck him. Vaguely he heard a collective gasp from the crowd—and a few shrieks—when the world suddenly exploded and he was plunged into a black nothingness.

Momentlessness engulfed him and he thought perhaps Hatfield had slain him after all. Then lights began to glow and whiz past him, stars and planets and glowing suns moving in a swirling kaleidoscope of color, until mist and clouds and whirling breezes surrounded him. Then the familiar smell of tulgey woods and TümTüm trees filled his nostrils, but even those faded and fled as white filled his vision: white banners and pillars and long flowing hair and the sweet scent of white chrysanthumoses. And lastly a voice of sweet whitish music fell upon his ears.

"Welcome home, my wondiferous hunter!" it murmured gently.

It? She! Luwys gazed up into the beautiful everyoung face of the White Queen. Standing beside her in the same glorious attire he had worn at MagnifiCon USA stood the Madgician smiling broadly. His bright colors contrasted somewhat madly with the white surroundings. "Indeed, my boy! Welcome back to Vündorlönde!" he said. "We couldn't have made it without you—or not, at least, without Vorpal!" The older man laid the sheathed weapon on the bed beside Luwys.

Luwys struggled to sit up, the room topsy-turving dangerously. He blinked and rubbed his head.

"There, there. No need to rush." The White Queen patted his hand and gently pushed him back into the softness of the white pillows and bedding. "My Madgician tells me world-hopping can leave a person feeling somewhat mimsy for a bit." She smiled. "You have slain the Bandersnatch, my hunter, and have returned my Madgician to me. And on this frabjous day, I name you, Luwys, son of Khaerel—Champion of the realm! And now, I'll leave you to rest." The white-clad queen rose elegantly from her perch on his bed and moved quietly out of the room.

Luwys watched her go, enraptured by her grace and beauty. He sighed happily, closing his eyes, which snapped back open at the Madgician's "Harrumph!"

Luwys blinked. "Sir?" he asked.

Hatfield bowed and leaned close. "Rest up, my boy! You might have slain the last of the Manxome Foes but there are plenty of frumious fiends to fight. Your days as a hunter have ended. Your days as a Champion have just begun! O, the adventures we'll have!" The Madgician chortled happily. "You with your Vorpal and me with my magic! But first . . ." Hatfield took off his large orange top hat and replaced it with a smaller green crushed velvet one. He grinned, holding up a cup and saucer. "Let's have some tea, shall we?"

The Lord of Iniriand

S. L. Rudder

L ord Telorin stood on the balcony of his sleeping chambers, overlooking the terrace garden below. He could see many Elves hurrying back and forth along the winding paths between the planting beds. All were busy with their duties and preparations: setting up tables, hanging lanterns, and arranging all manner of decorations. Living as he did in the middle of the Tharonwood, he tended to draw comparisons from nature. The dozens of Elves hurrying about their business below him looked more like a rushing brook than anything else. Having spent his fair share of time around Men, he reflected that if that race were involved, the scene below would more likely resemble a group of squirrels running about. He smiled as he thought, "Maybe that is why a group of squirrels is called a *scurry.*" With Elves it was not so. There was no wasted movement, no getting in each others' way or bumping into one another.

Everyone knew their job and did it well. To be fair, Elves had centuries more to practice working in tandem than Men did, and there were no novices working in the scene below him. The preparations they were handling were for the most important day of Lord Telorin's life; only masters of their craft would be touching anything today.

It had been decided more than a century earlier that an Elf Haven was needed deep in the Tharonwood because of the Enemy's increased activity in the region. The Elves had had an outpost there since the beginning of the age, with Telorin as its leader. The High Elves, along with the Council of Wizards, had decreed that more was needed. Telorin knew his company had done an excellent job protecting the 'Wood thus far and was eager to move forward with the added responsibilities. Iniriand would join Cirion in Astroth, Edaerioth in Brellonar, and Valamar in Pekka and become the fourth Elf Haven in Aaleria, and Telorin was proud to be named its ruler. As a full Haven, Telorin and his Elves would be much more able to help those travelling in his realm. Though the Havens were set up as places of safety and healing for the Elves, anyone in dire straits could find sanctuary in them—if they could find the Haven that is. No evil was allowed within the Havens' borders, and the scouts and rangers among the Elves protected the entire realm that held one.

Telorin had overseen every facet of Iniriand's construction as the Elven artisans worked to build a place of safety and beauty, and he was very satisfied with the outcome. Each Haven reflected the land where it abode, and in Iniriand, each type of tree or wood found in the forest was represented. The buildings and dwellings were built in and around living trees of enormous size, entire chambers carved inside the trunks in some cases. Every room or hall was paneled in rich, polished wood showing the color and grain of the many varieties at their very best. Not only were there innumerable pieces of hand carved furniture, the arches, beams, and supports were all carved to look like different trees and vines. Telorin had sent teams of Elves to harvest the 'Wood, collecting blown-down trees, reclaiming ones cut down by intruders, and thinning the growth to maintain the health of the forest. The Tharonwood was cared for as carefully as the Haven itself.

Telorin leaned on the railing of his balcony as he continued watching the preparations below. It was through strength of will that he did not make his way down there to hurry them along. "It would not do for the Lord of Iniriand to seem impatient," he said with a smile. To distract himself, he let his hand glide over the satin-like finish of the railing. The intertwined vines and flowers were so life-like, one almost expected to smell their perfume. He had the artisans use the same rich, warm wood here as in his sleeping quarters; it was finished in a deep, red tone, almost the color of new wine.

He turned from the terrace and made his way into the bed chamber. The tapestries and bed hangings here were shaded from a dusky rose to a deep violet. The counterpane on the bed itself was shot through with gold and silver threads causing it to sparkle in the firelight. Thick pillows were piled high at the head and soft furs were draped over the foot, waiting to chase off the chill on a cold winter's night. Stone taken from the rocky hills to the west of the Tharonwood tiled the floor and framed the large fireplace. The artisan's hand was seen here as well. The floor was smooth and perfectly fitted together with no crack or mortar showing. The fireplace was carved with every bird one might find in the 'Wood represented, their feathers shaped from inlaid colorful stones.

There were two doors, besides the ones to the terrace and out into the passageway, leading from the bed chamber. The one on the right opened into Telorin's study. It was decorated in shades of brown and green, reflecting the 'Wood that he loved so much. Cases filled with scrolls and books lined the walls, and two large tables covered in maps and papers stood on opposite sides of the room, with large, leather-clad chairs next to the hearth inviting one to sit and read. The study showed the Elf Lord's personality in every detail, but it did not draw him in this day.

With a smile shining in his green eyes, he crossed to the left-hand door and drew it open. Stepping inside, he let his eyes flow around the room, taking in each detail to make sure they were all perfect. This room was far different from his study, which was a picture of the 'Wood in all of its strength and glory. This room reflected the beauty of a quiet garden meadow and stream in the moonlight. In the four corners of the room were carved birch trees, their branches reaching up to meet overhead. Tapestries of wild flowers bloomed in muted shades between the birch trunks. Deep, shimmering carpets of teal and aqua covered the floor. The benches and chairs were in cool shades of lavender, blue, and green, with embroidery of silver threads throughout. Pillows of the same colors were scattered upon each seat. All the wooden pieces were whitewashed and polished to a silken shine.

Cases for scrolls and books were present here as well, but also cupboards and cabinets all carved to resemble bushes and trees lined the walls. A table and desk rounded out the furnishings of the room.

Telorin moved farther into the room and gazed up at the dozens of small lamps overhead. Each was made of pure silver with a pierced design that made them twinkle like stars. These Telorin had commissioned from the Dwarves of Drost. The silversmiths there were masters at their craft, which showed in the intricate beauty of each piece. Since they were Dwarven lamps, they were always glowing and never needed to be lit. He made his way over to the fireplace, the pleasure shining in his eyes. This too came from the Dwarves and was the centerpiece of the room. Carved from pure white marble, it looked like roses climbing a trellis. Each full blooming rose was set with precious stones; amethyst, ruby, sapphire, and topaz in a myriad of colors. When the fire was lit, the room would sparkle like a jewel box.

"This room is perfect in every way, except for one thing," Telorin mused to himself as he once more looked around. "It lacks a beautiful Elfess to enjoy it. That is a problem that will be remedied tonight." With a smile of anticipation spreading across his face, he left the chamber, quietly closing the door behind him, and made his way down and out to the terrace garden.

Iniriand was completed, ready for him to begin his rule. The dwellings and Halls were all finished and furnished. Flowers filled each garden and lined every winding pathway. Only one thing remained: the ruler of a Haven must have a spouse. Upon the formation of the first Haven, Kyrios had decreed that this would be so. As excited and proud as Telorin was to become the Lord of Iniriand, those feelings paled in comparison to the ones he felt when he thought of Celebriel and their marriage to come.

Telorin moved to a carved, high backed bench under an arbor hanging with wisteria. As he settled back into the corner, he gazed at a beautiful cluster of blossoms hanging near his face. His eyes were on the lavender petals, but his mind was far away in another garden long ago.

He had just returned to Valamar with a report of his command in the Tharonwood. Now, evening had fallen and he was taking a stroll along the flagstone pathways of a streamside garden. The garden opened out into a meadow filled with wildflowers of every shape and color imaginable, the whole scene silvered by the moonlight. He was wandering more or less aimlessly about, just enjoying the peace and beauty, when a slight movement caught his eye. There, just where the garden and meadow came together, was a trellis covered with climbing roses. The dew sparkled on the petals of each full bloom. Breathtaking as this was in the light of the full moon overhead, on this night it could not capture his eye.

Turning away from the trellis and walking toward the white stepping stones across the stream was the most beautiful Elfess he had ever seen! She held a perfect pink rose she had plucked from the trellis, and as she neared the water's edge, she brought it to her face, drinking in the fragrance. The cloud that had been partially covering the full moon overhead slipped aside and moonbeams flooded the scene before him. Telorin nearly forgot to breathe as the light washed over the Elfess. Her long, golden hair cascaded in waves down her back and shimmered in the light. She wore a pale blue and lavender dress that seemed to embrace the moonbeams and glow like a gossamer cloud stirring around her in the soft evening breeze.

"As I stand before the Lord Kyrios, you are the most beautiful vision I have ever seen!"

The unexpected voice startled the young Elfess, and she spun toward the speaker, dropping her rose as she did so, her hand flying to her throat.

Telorin stepped forward and bent to pick up the rose.

"Forgive me, my lady," he apologized, returning the bloom. "I did not mean to frighten you. I thought I was alone in the garden. When I saw you in the moonlight, I had to pay tribute. Your beauty is beyond compare." He bowed before her as she accepted the proffered flower.

"Thank you, my lord," she replied, her face glowing with a lovely blush as she did so. "I too thought I was alone in the garden."

"I will leave you to your solitude, if you wish," Telorin said as he made to turn away.

"No!" She placed a hand on his arm to stop him. Her blush deepened as she realized what she had done, and she dropped her hand back to her side. "I mean, it is a lovely evening, and I would enjoy sharing it with someone who appreciates its beauty as much as I do."

Telorin smiled. "That would be delightful. But first, I must know your name." He raised one eyebrow and tilted his head expectantly.

"Of course, my lord. My name is Celebriel."

Telorin reached up and plucked the wisteria blossom that he had been gazing at. He would never forget that night in the moon drenched garden. It was the first time he saw his beloved and knew in that moment that they were meant to be together. His thoughts returned to the present with a rush. Tonight under the moon in this garden he and Celebriel would wed! He nearly leaped from his seat, ready to rush out that very moment to claim his bride. Then he realized that the sun was still high overhead. There were hours to go before his wedding. What was he going to do to pass the time?

Just then, a hunting horn sounded. Guests were beginning to arrive.

"Good! Greeting travelers should fill in part of the time at least," he said as he started toward the Great Hall.

The kitchen mistress and one of her helpers were seeing to the table behind the arbor their Lord had been seated in. They shared smiles and even a small laugh. It was easy to see that the Lord Telorin's patience was near the breaking point. That fact did not bother them in the least. Everyone in the realm knew how deeply their lord loved his intended. They shared his joy and anticipation of the wedding to come.

Telorin had reached the Great Hall just as the first guests made their way inside. For many, this was their first sight of the new Haven, and there were many nods and comments on its beauty. The first company to arrive was Lady Tarithra's, from Edaerioth. Close behind her were the Elves of Cirion. Telorin's smile widened when he saw that Alendriel was with Lord Vilorin's company. The red-haired Elfess stepped forward to share a quick embrace. Many were the hunting trips the two had shared, and Telorin was delighted that she was here to share this day as well.

As he clasped the arms of fellow warriors and embraced relatives both near and distant, Telorin's eyes continued to drift to the tall double doors of the entrance.

"She is here, but you may not see her before the ceremony," spoke a soft voice in his ear.

"Indariel!" he bowed to the ruler of Valamar. "I was just checking to make sure the refreshments were sufficient for all my guests."

"Yes." A smile lit the eyes of the regal Elfess before him. "The honey cakes do look as if they are running low. You must rush right out to the kitchen and prepare some more."

Telorin answered that comment with a burst of laughter. "I fear you know me much too well."

"Yes, but you are still young. Patience comes with age." The smile spread to Indariel's face. "There is still hope you might gain more."

Telorin laughed once more. "Yes, but Elves are supposed to be born with that virtue, are we not?"

Just then, the horn of greeting sounded once more.

"Forgive me, my Lady, I do believe the wizards have arrived. I must see to their comfort."

"I well understand." Indariel inclined her head in dismissal, her eyes still sparkling with merriment. "Wizards are not known for their patience either."

* * * *

The hour had finally come. All of the guests were seated, the lanterns were lit and sparkling overhead, and the head of the Wizards' Council was waiting on the raised dais in front of a rose covered trellis at the far end of the garden. Telorin stood beside him, clothed in robes of the deepest forest green. He was willing himself to stand patiently as he awaited the arrival of his bride.

Just when he thought he had reached his limit, the full moon lifted over the canopy of trees and flooded the guests with its light, the large double doors to the Great Hall opened, and lovely Elven music played by unseen musicians began drifting through the garden. As the beautiful strains of music swelled forth, two columns of Elves bearing lanterns on poles circled around the west tower of the Great Hall and into the garden. As the head of each column reached the open area around the dais, they came to a halt and turned to face each other, their lanterns creating a trail of lights.

When the lighted path had been formed, two young Elflings made their way around the tower and toward the dais, each carrying a blue velvet pillow. The young Elf lass' burden was covered with a silver cloth, the lad's with a cloth of gold. They made their way to the foot of the dais, paused to bow before Lord Telorin and the Wizard, then made their ways to the opposite corners and took their places facing the guests. When they were in place, a second pair of Elflings came into view bearing a large, deep purple pillow between them. Resting on this was the golden Elven wedding cord, its two ends coiled on opposite sides and gleaming in the light of the lanterns. These bearers also bowed in respect and remained at the foot of the steps, facing Telorin and the Wizard.

Telorin stopped himself from taking a step forward in anticipation. He caught Indariel and Alendriel sharing knowing smiles out of the corner of his eye. He silently upbraided himself as he resumed his stance beside the Wizard, trying to make himself relax. He knew that Celebriel would be the next one to come around the tower. It was a sight he was longing for.

The music paused, and then began again in even more ethereal tones. Around the corner came the nose of a lovely bay mare, caparisoned all in silver. As the horse took another step, Celebriel came into view. Even among Elves, her beauty stood out. She was dressed in a pale blue silk gown, covered with silver lace, the moonbeams and lanterns causing her to appear to glow. All eyes in the Garden were fixed on her lovely face. The beautiful bride had eyes only for her groom, and when their eyes met, both felt that time itself stopped for just a moment.

The mare continued on up to the steps of the dais. One of Telorin's honor guards stepped up to help the bride down. As she mounted the steps, looking at him with eyes filled with love, Telorin released the breath he did not know he had been holding. He longed to rush forward and clasp her in his arms, but knew that he must wait. If he could have read her thoughts in that moment, he would have known she shared his feelings, but the Elven wedding protocols were ages old and must be followed.

The Wizard stepped forward and held his staff out between Telorin and Celebriel. The young couple each placed their hands on the staff, Telorin's outside his bride's, and bowed their heads.

"Lord Kyrios," the Wizard prayed, "may You bless the joining of Telorin and Celebriel. May each of us who witness this union grant them help and strength in the journey they are about to begin. May Your blessing follow them through this life and into the one to come."

The Wizard lowered his staff, and the couple crossed and joined their hands, right to right and left to left. The young cord bearers climbed the steps and raised their pillow. Handing his staff to the waiting attendant, the Wizard lifted the coil nearest Celebriel and wound it around the couple's clasped hands, binding them together. He then repeated this action with the second coil.

"Telorin," the Wizard spoke as he turned to the Elf. "Do you promise to care for Celebriel, to love her, protect her, and provide for her as long as Kyrios gives you breath?"

Telorin looked deep into the eyes of his bride, a smile lighting his face. "I do swear."

The Wizard gave a nod, and then turned to the bride. "Do you, Celebriel, promise to care for Telorin, to love him, serve him, and help him as long as Kyrios gives you breath?"

Celebriel's face was aglow as she spoke so softly she could barely be heard. "I do so swear."

The Wizard nodded once more as he then placed his left hand on the bound hands of the couple before him and raised his right above their bowed heads.

"As this golden cord binds the hands of these Your servants, may You bind their hearts in purity, beauty, and strength. May they ever serve You, Lord Kyrios, and may they light the way for all the children You may bless them with."

The Wizard stepped back and retrieved his staff. Placing the head of the staff on top of the golden cord, he spoke once more.

"By the Lord Kyrios, I join these two souls, both now and for Eternity!"

The staff and the hands of the couple were engulfed in a brilliant flash of light. When the light faded away,

Telorin and Celebriel stood before the Wizard, each with a golden band around their left wrist. Telorin's was a heavy rope cuff, and Celebriel's was a delicate set of intertwined bangles.

"Now, you may embrace your bride," the Wizard gave Telorin a knowing smile.

When the newly married couple separated, a cheer swelled from the guests.

"Enough of that," the Wizard ordered, trying to sound gruff and banging his staff against the floor. "Our work here is not finished yet.

"Will the Wizards of the Council and the High Elves please join me?"

When all had taken their places, the young Elflings with the blue pillows stepped forward and mounted to the top step of the dais.

"Not only have we come here this evening to join Lord Telorin and Lady Celebriel in marriage, we are also here to officially make them rulers of this new Haven of Iniriand."

The cloths were removed from the pillows to reveal a golden circlet on the one and a silver circlet on the other. The Elf couple knelt before him and the Wizard placed the silver on Celebriel's brow, and the gold on Telorin's.

When this was accomplished, he held out his hands over their bowed heads, his staff above Telorin.

"Do you swear before the Lord Kyrios, this Council, the High Elves, and all gathered here to rule this Haven according to the laws set down in the Book of Adonai, to protect and succor all within your borders, and to defend your realm against all the forces of Evil?"

"We so swear," the couple spoke in unison.

"Rise and face your subjects." The Wizard spread his arms wide behind the smiling pair before him.

"I give you the Lord and Lady of Iniriand. May they rule with wisdom, compassion, and honor, and may the blessing and protection of Kyrios cover this Haven from now until the end of time."

A cheer was raised by all present, followed by a night of feasting, joy, and celebration.

Jonathan M. Rudder

Dynamic: A New Reality

Jonathan M. Rudder

The cavern walls flickered with the multi-hued glow of the magical fire heating the forge at the center of the chamber. The forge itself was an impractical cauldron of gold, ringed with spiked bands of silver. Silver horns of various sizes rose up from the lip of the over-glorified kettle.

Before the blazing forge, the Magesmith Validar stood, arms raised before him, face uplifted, eyes closed. His lips moved with the intonation of his spell, his baritone voice, echoing through the chamber above the roar of the forge. He was so close to achieving his finest creation, a creation that would save the world . . . a world that had set itself on a path of inevitable doom.

His creation would prepare the way for the purest of heart and mind to bring order back into the world. It would not be a short, swift process. He deemed it would take years before the world would be ready.

A white light began to form within the rainbow tongues licking forth from the forge, a ball of luminescence that began to distort and twist in upon itself. The white light shattered into seven clear crystals, hovering between the horns of the forge. Slowly, each one began to fill with color. Red, orange, and yellow, green and blue, violet. . . .

A distant voice pierced through the veil of Validar's mind, calling to him from beyond the Magescape. He tried to block out the persistent noise. He could not tolerate the distraction now, at the end of his labors. He struggled to maintain focus.

The seventh crystal shuddered. It wanted life, but the spectrum had already given itself to the other six crystals. Validar focused on the seventh crystal. He could feel it in his mind. He knew what it needed.

What are you doing? There's only three hours left. . . !

The voice was growing louder. Validar was losing his grasp on the crystal. Summoning the last of his strength, he screamed out the last line of his spell. "*Selected target dot renderer dot material dot color equals color dot black!*"

The seventh crystal slowly misted over, brown, then murky grey, then black. The crystal seemed to emanate a black aura, difficult to imagine, but present nonetheless.

Frank, you in there?

Validar smiled and opened his eyes. The cavern around him began to swirl and fragment, disintegrating in a cloud of multi-colored sparkles. . . .

Frank Valentine removed the small devices from his temples, and the blinking multi-colored lights ringing them went dark. He blinked and sat still for a moment, allowing his five natural senses to readjust to the real world.

He looked up at Bob Gurrie, his office-mate. "Hey, Bob. Just finalizing a little bit of code. Almost done."

Bob's large, hazel eyes seemed to almost pop out of his gaunt face in disbelief. "What? If Nora knew you were messing with live code this close to launch, you'd be looking for a new job."

Frank smiled sweetly. "Nah, she's my fiancé. Anyway, I found a critical bug the beta-testers appear to have missed. It's a blocker. If I don't get it cleaned up, the world's going to crash like nothing you've ever seen."

Bob leaned on the desk, agape. "Seriously?"

Frank dipped his head in response. "And as you pointed out, there's only three hours left. . . ."

"Get to it then!" Bob said, flicking his fingers at Frank. "I'll let Nora know what's up."

Frank nodded. "You do that."

As Bob hurried out the office door, Frank glanced back over his shoulder and grimaced. This was an unforeseen problem, but he would have to address it later. Right now, he had to finish his work. The world—the *real* world—depended on it.

He knew no one would understand. Maybe Nora—though he expected she would also misinterpret his motives, like everyone else. His goals were to preserve and protect the future of the human race, and this code would do just that.

As Frank stuck the small devices against his temples, and the indicator lights began to flash once more, he smirked. It was ironic that the fate of the world depended on a video game.

After a brief electrical sting from the conduits, Frank found himself drawn back into the Magescape, entering his avatar, Validar, digitally projected into his mind— a nearly perfect image of himself—still standing before the forge at the center of the cavern . . . only the cavern had changed. A few dim torches flickered in the chamber, all that remained of any light sources. The forge lay in ruins before him, the crystals gone.

Validar frantically dug through the rubble in a panic, but there was no doubt: the crystals had been taken.

What could have happened? Validar's eyes narrowed. *Betas!*

There must have been a crack in the physics he had placed at the cavern entrance. It was a development area . . . no one except a dev was supposed to have access. In this case, he was the only one who knew the location. He had coded precautions against his co-workers discovering the space.

His brow beetling in wrath, Validar arose and thrust out his hand. A wizard's staff resolved in his grasp. As he marched towards the cavern entrance, he used every dev command he knew to summon the rarest and most powerful gear and artifacts into his possession. His black robes swirled around him and reformed into black plate armor, encrusted with glowing gems and trimmed with intricate designs in silver. His black cloak shifted to blood-red, embroidered with silver designs. Rings of various metals, studded with various gems, appeared on every finger. A medallion, belt, and other accouterments also appeared.

As he stepped into the light outside the cavern, he looked around. The lush forest surrounding the grassy knoll, which concealed his vast lair, could not hide the presence of the invaders. Between dev tools and in-game gear, he was able to locate the entire party. Foolishly, they had encamped only fifty yards away in a small clearing.

Validar strode through the forest, his cloak billowing behind him.

As he emerged into the clearing, he saw a band of seven adventurers gathered around a campfire. They were distributing their loot—*his* belongings—among themselves. Despite his lack of stealth, they did not seem to notice him at once. He quickly appraised the party.

Mercenary, Paladin, Wizard, Ranger, Thief, Wound-taker, Brute, he thought. *Basic classes . . . not even a multiclasser. Pitiful.*

"I think you have a few things that belong to me," Validar rumbled, raising his staff before him.

The adventurers started at his voice. Each and every one of them gawked at his advanced gear. Finally, the Paladin found his voice.

"Who art thou? The master of the fell lair yonder? Arise, my friends . . . methinks we have stumbled upon a chance encounter with a legendary figure!"

Great, Validar groaned inwardly. *An RPer.*

He snarled aloud, "I'll give you *legendary*."

He thrust his empty hand towards the Paladin and uttered a single word in the Magetongue. A bolt of crimson fire erupted from his splayed fingers and blew a hole through the Paladin's chest.

"Man," the Minotaur Brute grunted. "That is soooo bogus. No blood. I hate these kid-friendly games."

"I knew we should have brought a Cleric," whined the Woundtaker. "I don't have anything to rez him with."

Validar blinked in disbelief. "Are you serious? I just one-shotted your most powerful party member . . . and you're going to sit there and rant about the game?"

"Um, guys," the Elfess Ranger started slowly. "I don't think he's a mob."

"Dude!" the green-skinned Mercenary exclaimed in unbridled excitement. "How'd you get the dope gear? Promo code?"

So the Paladin was the only RPer. I'm not sure which is more annoying. . . .

"I created it," Validar intoned in a low voice.

"I didn't know you could craft that stuff," the Human Wizard returned.

Validar's lip curled into a sneer. "*You* can't."

He raised his hands in the air and recited a brief spell. Electricity played between his fingertips, growing into a complex web of blue lightning.

When the adventurers realized what was happening, they turned and scattered . . . but too late. Validar brought his hands down before him, and bolts of blue lightning lashed out, forking towards the fleeing party. One by one, each of the adventurers fell in a smoking ruin.

Validar stepped forward and searched the corpses, withdrawing a gem from each. As he placed the last one in his satchel, he frowned. The black crystal was still missing!

Understanding dawned upon him as his eyes darted across the clearing. The Thief was gone. *She must have ducked into the shadows.*

He surveyed the corpses around him. *I'll have to deal with these idiots first.*

"If you haven't already guessed," he said to the motionless bodies. "I'm a dev. You knowingly exploited a bug in a development zone to obtain powerful, unfinished items. I'm going to be lenient, however, since the stolen goods have been recovered. Your accounts will be frozen until live release in two and a half hours.

"You may, of course, file an appeal, but given the nature of the offense, I do not recommend it."

Validar waved his hand, and the corpses faded away. *That should buy me enough time.*

He reached into his satchel and withdrew the six gems he had recovered. With a sweep of his hand, he released them into the air before him, where they hung like tiny stars.

Each one had its own unique power. Each one represented a different human trait necessary to bring the world out of the morass humanity had made of it. Each one was, in effect, a key. Those who learned their secret, who could control their power, would be the ones to inherit the Earth.

"It's time to do your job," he muttered to the crystals. Validar lifted his hand again and swept it first one way, and then the other. The six gems shot off in different directions, vanishing from his view.

He smiled to himself. Of course, the gems were also the locks that needed to be opened. A flicker of annoyance crossed his features. The black gem was vital. It was the master stone. It needed to be inserted into a key system to activate.

Now, he thought. *To find the Thief. Locate spell won't work. Have to cheat. What was her name. . . ?*

With a nod of remembrance, Validar raised both hands before him. "Slash devmenu space open bracket playerlocate pound Niberia close bracket. Send."

A map of the Magescape appeared before him, with a red dot blinking in the vicinity of the nearest town. *Gotcha.*

* * * *

The Human Thief Niberia stood in a shadowy corner of the Revina Bazaar, holding the faceted black crystal up before her. "So what are you? Crafting material? Vendor trash? Doubt that. This looks like a Unique of some kind."

Niberia pulled back her hood, revealing a young teen with a tangled mess of auburn hair and a dirty face. She stepped out of the shadows and strode up to the nearest vendor. "Can you identify this?"

The large, balding NPC looked at it for half a second, then shook his head. "I am not familiar with that object. It is of no discernable use."

Niberia shook her head. *Need to hire a better dialogue writer.*

"Vendor trash then," she sighed. "Mighty fancy vendor trash, though. Wonder if it will net me a platinum?"

She held it out to the vendor again. "I want to sell this."

The vendor took the crystal and held it up. He shook his head and handed it back. "This item may not be sold or traded."

Niberia raised a brow. "Really?"

She shook her head. "Typical. Can't sell it, trade it, give it away, or use it for anything. Buggy game. Can't believe they're launching it today."

With a sigh, Niberia tossed the black crystal into a sewer drain and watched it dematerialize into the void of the deletion pool.

* * * *

Validar watched Niberia toss the crystal into the sewer. His lip quirked. *Thank you, Thief. That will do just fine. Three . . . two . . . one. . . .*

The game world pixelated and vanished.

Frank opened his eyes and let them readjust. He smiled to himself. In twenty minutes, the Magescape would reinitialize, and half a billion pre-purchased keys would be activated. He removed the conduits from his head and rested them on the desk before him.

"Frank," a woman's voice said behind him.

Frank's hands wrapped around the conduits and slid from the desktop. He turned to face the speaker, a smile stretching across his lips. "Hey, Beautiful! Ready for the Great Flood?"

Nora Fletcher, *Magescape*'s Executive Producer, frowned. "Frank, Bob said you discovered a blocker and were working on a fix. . . ."

Frank stood up and thrust his hands into his pants' pockets, allowing the conduits to drop inside. "Yeah, there was an issue with the player portal. I've taken care of it. I just need to run down to the server room and make an adjustment to the world shard."

Nora looked worried. "Do you think you can resolve the issue in less than fifteen minutes?"

"Not if I'm standing here," Frank replied with a wink. "Be right back."

He stepped toward his fiancé and gave her a quick peck on the cheek. As he slipped past her and out the door, he breathed a sigh of relief.

Frank rushed through the Dynamic Studios facility to the server room. He swiped his key card across the lock and slipped inside. He glanced at the other release engineers, then slipped into a chair before a terminal and quickly logged in. His fingers flew across the keyboard, while he bemoaned the inability to access the game code through the conduits.

When he was done, he hit <enter> and waited, eyes glued on the computer's clock. The final two minutes seemed to take an eternity. Sweat beaded on his forehead. If anyone discovered his changes, they could lock down the launch. The gems would not activate until the game reinitialized.

Noon rolled around at last, and *Magescape* made its public debut. Frank watched with growing elation as the player count rose astronomically.

In less than five minutes, the other engineers started to rush around in a panic.

"The entire game . . . it's transferring to another shard!" one fellow called out.

"Kick the players," the supervisor replied, his voice strained.

The first one banged at a keyboard, then said, "I can't! The game has locked me out!"

"Track it! Which backup shard?"

The engineer shook his head, thunderstruck. "None of them. The shard . . . it isn't ours."

The supervisor's eyes widened. "What's the address?"

"I don't know . . . I've never seen anything like this!"

"You'd better figure it out . . . there are nearly five-hundred million minds trapped in that game."

The engineer keyed in a command, then swallowed. "Boss . . . you better take a look."

The supervisor cursed as he viewed the engineer's screen. "How did this happen? What kind of demented mind could have done this? Call Ms. Fletcher. We've got a crisis on our hands. . . ."

As the supervisor read the message he had planted, Frank smiled, gently slipping the conduits from his pockets. He had done it. Stage one of his plan to save the human race from itself had succeeded.

His dream was becoming a reality . . . a world-changing reality.

Message Received

S. L. Rudder

Communications Detection/Translation Engineer 11B was hard at work at his station. The young junior officer was going over print-outs and comparing data between his techpad and the large shipboard tech screen readouts. From the appearance of his station, no one would realize the internal chaos he was dealing with. Every paper, instrument, and electrical part was in perfect order. Nothing was askew. Nothing was misplaced. Most of all, nothing was dropped on the floor or scattered around. The outward appearance made it seem as if he had everything under perfect control. That appearance was far from true. The simple fact was that CD/TE11B was a Vlivlarian. Having everything in its appropriate place was hardwired into his DNA. The only jumbles and disorder he would tolerate at all were the ones in his own mind, and he was working hard to eliminate those as well.

Vlivlarians were the most advanced people in the known universe, in all areas. They were an extremely artistic people, but they required symmetry and continuity in everything, leading CD/TE11B to want to get his thoughts straightened out and under control. Like all of his race, his desire for order and balance in all things made him an extremely good problem solver. While his talent dealt with communications transmitters and receivers, the same trait, along with the ability to understand other races, made his people highly efficient diplomats. Their artistry could be seen in the flowing, curving lines of their ships' design, ships that boasted weapons and defensive systems powerful enough to handle any hostile race they might encounter.

Even though the Space League of Worlds had been formed centuries ago, CD/TE11B still found it difficult sometimes to deal with the startling differences between the races involved. Because of this diversity, the SLW worked to make sure that differences were overcome without any race losing their individuality. Still, many adjustments had to be made along the way to allow all members of the League to work together. Some of these were harder than others.

CD/TE11B had just finished his training at the academy on Vlivlary two years ago, and this was his first posting. So far, for him, the hardest thing to deal with was the fact that other races used their given names. This was in direct opposition to his Vlivlarian upbringing. In his culture, each individual goes by their designation, which can change many times in a lifespan. Take CD/TE11B himself for example. Communications Detection/Translations Engineer was his expertise and field of study. The "11" was his section on the Communications deck. The "B" was his designation in the rotation for his unit or team. The Vlivlarian military units were most often set up in multiples of four. Thus CD/TE11B was the second in rotation of his unit of four engineers. His given name was only known by three individuals: himself and his parents. If he chose to take a lifemate someday, then she would also be told. Names were too intimate to be known by all and were guarded as sacred treasures. In some younger, more "progressive" families, siblings might also know each other's names, but for CD/TE11B, as with most established families, that was not the case.

Mainly due to the Vlivlarian's thirst for knowledge, the SLW sent out many probes and starships in ever expanding circles from their own sector of the galaxy. One of these advanced Vlivlarian long-range/extended study starships was where CD/TE11B found himself. Their goal was to find new races in the hope of bringing them into the SLW. Nothing was done in haste. When a new race was found, they would be studied through the scans received by the long-range starships and the probes they launched. This practice kept the SLW from approaching beings that were not ready psychologically or emotionally to make outside first contacts. It also helped avoid contact with races that were too hostile or aggressive.

The Vlivlarians were not interested in conquest. The peaceful approach was always their first choice. If that failed, CD/TE11B knew he still had little to worry about. They had yet to come up against a race they could not have conquered in a military encounter if that had been their desire. It was not. They only desired to add worlds to the League which had something of worth to contribute, or worlds and races that they could aid themselves.

The first choice was always study and observation, then contact if a race was deemed ready. If the new beings failed to pass the set criteria, the SLW's policy was a simple withdrawal. That race would never even know that they had been under observation.

One of the best ways to study a possible new member race was through their communications. That was where CD/TE11B and his team came in. The enormous variety of worlds and cultures in the galaxy led the Vlivlarians to constantly make advances in their transmitting and receiving technology as well as their translations computer. CD/TE11B lived and worked on the communications deck of a starship two sectors from his home system of Vlivlary. The ship's mission was to study all inhabited planets in their assigned region. All transmissions and communications had to be examined to determine when, or even if, contact would be made with any given race—which made CD/TE11B's job so important and exciting. His team of console engineers developed the equipment used to detect and monitor any new form of communications they came across. They worked in tandem with the observer/listener techs who monitored every form of communications at the receiver/transmitter banks. These banks had units to record any broadcasts or communications they picked up in their area of space. A Communications Detection/Translation Engineer's job was at its most exciting if they were able to discover new wavelengths. Unfortunately, this did not happen very often. If any such discovery was made, he and his team would need to design and build new units so that the communications could be studied. Receiving communications you could not understand would be a waste of time and effort, which meant the engineers were also constantly upgrading the translation computer's programming, allowing it to "learn" new languages as needed. The timetable for decoding a new language varied greatly depending on how closely it might resemble the known languages in the database.

The chaos that CD/TE11B was dealing with was the fact that he believed he had discovered a new wavelength, and he was working round the clock to gather all the evidence he could to support his discovery. He had, of course, reported the first anomalous reading he found the week prior. At that point he had not realized what he might have found. Each subsequent night since then, he had been reporting more anomalous readings. His theory that he had found a new wavelength grew with each new report. He had compiled data from all of his team members' reports, studied printouts, and recorded all evidence. Some points he found were so miniscule they had been overlooked initially. In fact, some he would not have noticed himself if he had not known what to look for.

"I am told that you have made an interesting discovery."

The unexpected voice of his SubCommander caused CD/TE11B to slide out of his chair and come to attention, each movement of his slender frame graceful and smooth. His elongated, pointed ears turned from the yellow/white of surprise to the light pink of embarrassment. The Vlivlarians' facial expressions were difficult for other races to read, but it did not take long to learn to judge their emotions by their "ear response." Being a Vlivlarian, CD/TE11B had no trouble reading the face of his SubCommander standing before him. The older Vlivlarian was as close to laughter as their race ever came, a fact reinforced by the rosy color of her ears.

"My Senior SubCommander 11 tells me you have discovered a new wavelength," she stated as she took a seat in front of his work station and waved the young engineer back into his own chair.

"As I stated in my report, SubCommander, I believe there is every possibility that I have." He passed his techpad to the senior officer as he turned the pile of printed readouts to face her. "I have been going over all the findings for the last week. As you can see from the data on this techpad, and from the image comparisons on the tech screen, there is something we are receiving that does not fit any of our known wavelengths. None of our instruments can identify it, but, if you will allow me . . ." He rose and moved around the desk beside the SubCommander.

"Do you see this reading, here, here, and here?" He waited as she studied the areas he had noted before continuing. "Now, if you would watch the tech screen, beginning with these data images from a week ago, observe the frames I have highlighted. The images in these frames are multiplied by 73.84 percent."

Slowly, letting each image remain on the tech screen for several seconds, CD/TE11B moved through the slides until he reached the images for the previous day.

"There is an unexplained line or smudge in each of the frames," the SubCommander noted.

"Yes! For lack of a better term, we have been calling it a shadow reading."

"That seems an appropriate term," she agreed. "It does appear to shadow the other image. Each day, the shadow has grown larger."

"Correct, but they remain nearly undetectable without magnification. At first it was thought to be a misalignment or other technical malfunction. After running a complete diagnostic analysis of the entire system, the shadow remained. We have run daily diagnostics checks for the past week, yet the shadow remains and, as you noted, has increased.

"These are today's images." He switched the screen once more. "There are two more frames showing a slight 'shadow.' And when I switch off the magnification . . ."

"The highest frame now shows the minute shadow." She placed the techpad back on the desk and looked through the paper readouts, carefully studying each notation. "Your hypothesis is that you are detecting an unknown wavelength that is growing in strength. I must admit, I agree with this hypothesis. Your report stated that you were designing a new receiver."

"Yes, SubCommander," he said, his excitement showing as his ears shaded from pale yellow at the bottom to pink at the tips. "We have finished the preliminary schematics. The parts specifications have been sent to replication/production. As you can see, I have begun assembling the computer core already."

Remembering well the excitement of one's first discovery, the SubCommander rose and prepared to leave the young engineer to his work. "I will be awaiting your reports and am eager to follow your progress."

"Thank you, SubCommander. I hope I do not disappoint."

"I have no such fear, Communications Detection/ Translations Engineer 11B. Continue as you were."

For the next several days, CD/TE11B and his team worked to complete the new unit. Then, just as they were ready to install and test it, the shadow reading began to grow fainter.

Once again, CD/TE11B began poring over data and readouts. It did not take him long to discover that the strength of the shadow readings growing fainter corresponded with the spaceship's change of course.

"The signal must be directional, or else very short range," he mused, busily making notations to include in his evening report. He was careful to supply his Sub-Commander with copies of all the data showing the exact correlation between the ship's course and the strength of the shadow reading.

Upon receipt and review of the report, the Ship Commander ordered a return to the previous course. To the delight of CD/TE11B and his team, as soon as the course correction was implemented, the shadow readings grew stronger once more.

The next day, under the supervision of the Communications Senior SubCommander, CD/TE11B and his team installed the newly completed receiving unit.

"Communications Detection/Translation Engineers 11 A to D, is your new unit ready for its first live trial?"

All four console engineers lowered their heads in acknowledgement.

"Very well, you may begin operations immediately." The Senior SubCommander seated himself at the desk provided to observe the operation.

The results were more than CD/TE11B could have

hoped for. Line after line of unreadable text began scrolling across the data screen of the unit. His ears were nearly strobing from yellow to pink as he watched Observer/Listener 11C key in the record command on the translations computer and the machine began its "learning" process. O/L11A linked the new unit with the wall-mounted tech screen enabling all to see the messages as they were being recorded.

"Most laudable, CD/TE11," the SubCommander rose and moved to inspect the tech screen more closely. He turned to face the elated young team. "What designation have you given your new wavelength?"

The entire team looked to CD/TE11B in expectation. It had been his discovery, and they had unanimously agreed that he should be the one to name it.

"We are calling them sub-krontomic waves," he spoke, with pride clearly showing in his ears.

"Yes, that is quite logical. The krontom receiver was the first to detect the shadow. Very good. It will be so noted in the logs." After a few more minutes of observation, the SubCommander made his way to the door. "Carry on. I will be watching your reports and will return when the translation computer has mastered this new language. This is the first new wavelength discovered in three generations. There will be commendations for each member of the team added to your files."

CD/TE11B logged the strength of the signal. When it was clear enough that there were no breaks in the received transmissions, he notified the bridge, as ordered. The ship was brought to a halt, in order to avoid detection, and probes were sent out to pinpoint their point of origin. Data flowed into the bridge for the next two weeks from those probes to be dealt with by the appropriate units and personnel. CD/TE11B and his colleagues were hard at work in communications.

The translation computer was beginning to make progress with the new language. CD/TE11B was encouraged by this, but he wanted more. He was hoping to pick up an audio or visual message. Now that he knew he had helped find a new race, he wanted to know what they sounded and looked like. After many failed attempts and adjustments, he and his team had to conclude that text based communications were all that this new race used. CD/TE11's new transmitter/receiver was capable of sending and receiving all forms of transmissions, but evidently this new people's was not. CD/TE11B hoped that if and when communications were set up, he could give this new race instruction on modifying their units. The computer was beginning to translate small snippets of text and the more he was able to understand, the more he wondered about the beings sending the messages.

As they entered their second month of observation, when he was not on translation computer duty, CD/TE11B could be found poring over all the probe data available. The closer the computer got to decoding the transmissions, the less he slept. He spent all of his time looking for something that might give him a clue about this new race. His mind was so full of speculation as to who they were and what they looked like, he even dreamed about the possibilities when he finally did seek his bed for a few hours rest.

CD/TE11B was very imaginative; waking or sleeping his brain whirled with ideas. Were these people tall and willowy like the Vlivlarians? Or were they short and stout? Was their skin close in color and appearance to the polished ivory of his people? Or were they more colorful, or perhaps dark and matte? Did they have silken, silver hair as he did? Or could they be covered in scales, feathers or fur? These questions troubled his mind, and until they made contact—if they made contact—he had no way of knowing. If only they had some holographic or other visual communications that could be intercepted! The small chance that he might never know was a thought that he pushed far from his mind. At this point, he was not sure he could deal with that idea.

Finally, two and a half months after receiving the first message, CD/TE11B happened to be on duty when the computer made a significant breakthrough. He was so ecstatic that he nearly forgot to log the report. Even though most were only partial translations, he keyed to have them all sent to his techpad as they were decoded. His ears switching from excitement to anticipation, he would pore over every one, desperately searching for any clue to the species they were monitoring.

The young engineer could not count the times he had fallen asleep at the desk in his quarters going over the charts and data from the ship's probes since they had located the system of origin for his signal. It was a ten planet system containing two inhabited worlds. Three of the moons orbiting the larger of these had colonies of their own. The current theory was that this larger planet was also the capital of the system since it was the central location of the transmissions they intercepted.

The information the probes discovered intrigued CD/TE11B. This race apparently never travelled outside their system. Ships of all sizes passed back and forth between the various settlements, but no ship even approached the outer boundary. Another interesting fact was that the Vlivlarian probes were the only ones in the system. From all appearances, this was a race with very little curiosity about the universe that surrounded them. They were totally contained in their system, and were content to stay that way. CD/TE11B tried not to worry that this behavior would cause Command to deem them not ready for contact.

His worries were eased for the moment when the probes were moved into closer orbit of the system. At this new distance they could gather much more detailed data. Suddenly, CD/TE11B was looking at images of croplands, settlements, and buildings! Much to his chagrin, there were no clear images of the population as yet, just small beings hard at work at various tasks.

The more data that came in, the more CD/TE11B wanted to know. His colleagues began comparing him to an expectant parent, and he was forced to agree with them. Every time his techpad would signal a new data dump, he would snatch it up, ears again strobing from pale yellow to pink in excitement of what he might learn. Regardless of the fact that they were all receiving the same data, he felt the need to point out each and every fascinating point to his teammates. The others could not complain too much. They were nearly as excited as he was and realized that if this had been their "find" they would have been just as bad.

Just when his anticipation seemed to be at its very limit, the translations computer came up with a name for the race: "Dylintari." CD/TE11B was so relieved by this fact that at the end of his watch he fell straight into his bunk and slept the entire twelve hours until he was due back on duty.

With the discovery of the Dylintari's name, the translation computer seemed to sort out all of its problems, and filled in the blanks on all the previous messages. CD/TE11B was nearly overwhelmed going over these, along with the new probe data that came in. He spent every spare moment he had glued to his techpad and keying up image after image on the tech screen. Sometimes the other engineers almost feared they would not be able to get their own work done because of it, but they too wanted to know as much as they could. A picture of the race began forming through the images and data. Not a picture of them physically—that problem was still driving CD/TE11B to distraction—but a picture of their culture.

Through his study, CD/TE11B came to see that the Dylintari were a peaceful people. They were not nearly as advanced as the Vlivlarians in most areas. Their ships were not designed to handle deep space travel, but were more than capable for the work they carried out in system. He found that their manufacturing was very limited in scope. The main things they built were designed to aid in the primary function of the species. The Dylintari were farmers, and rather amazing and advanced at their craft. Different groups specialized in different aspects of farming. Some grew crops in open fields, while others operated large hydroponic farms. There were large collections and great varieties of herd animals, both free-ranging and in specifically designed enclosures. From going through reports, CD/TE11B found that the animals were not just used for food but also for a great range of other purposes.

The young engineer was especially intrigued by the images and specs of the food processing facilities. These were highly advanced. In fact, the colonies on the second moon specialized in nothing else. All of the Dylintari's farming varied greatly by location. Each settlement, whether on planet or moon, specialized in its own form of agricultural endeavors.

The data CD/TE11B downloaded from the probes came at an amazing rate. The data files were full of statistics, readouts, and schematics of every building and vehicle within the probes' range. He was nearly overwhelmed by the exquisite detail, both form and color, of the flora and fauna. But, to his regret, there were no clear pictures of the Dylintari themselves. The images indicated that their physical structure and size was quite similar to the Vlivlarians, but you still could not tell what they looked like. No matter where they were living or working, the Dylintari people were completely covered, faces included. No matter the climate—jungle, desert, or arctic—they all wore similar coverings. The fabrics differed in weight and color, but the design was almost identical. Almost like uniforms of some kind, he thought. He could understand this type of thinking; it was very close to the way his own people operated. When you discovered the best tool or design to fit the job, you did not change it without good reason. The Dylintari just seemed to carry the idea a little bit to the extreme where clothing was concerned. Somehow, thinking that they might have something in common made him feel a little bit closer to them.

Now that there were no longer any blank spaces in the messages he received, CD/TE11B felt he knew the

Dylintari a little more each day as he read them. Most of the communications had to do with their agricultural pursuits. There were delivery schedules for crops and animal shipments, reports on weather and growing conditions, all the messages you would expect farmers to send to one another.

While these could be fascinating, and CD/TE11B studied every one, he enjoyed the personal messages so much more. He was learning so many wonderful things from these which increased his desire to contact this race exponentially. One of his most interesting discoveries was that most family units seemed to stay in the same hub or settlement. A few messages he read indicated that this was not always the case. Sometimes family members sent messages between different hubs. He came to the conclusion that this happened when Dylintari took lifemates from outside their own settlement. The engineer could not prove this, despite his endless study, but he felt it was the most logical explanation.

Hidden away among the business and personal communiqué, CD/TE11B infrequently found items more official in nature. He came across government rulings and actions, and even less frequently, settlements of disputes. Few of these could be qualified as true legal issues, but each one was handled in a very forthright manner. The Dylintari were a society that expected everyone to live in harmony and work for the betterment of the whole. The punishment for those who caused turmoil or damage of any sort was swift and fitting to the crime. Again this caused the engineer to draw comparisons with his own people.

All the similarities he found were character based. When it came to technological advancement, the contrast was stark. Every message re-enforced the picture of a simple, peace-loving, agricultural race. It was this simplicity that fascinated CD/TE11B the most. It was a fascination that the entire ship's crew was coming to share. When duty allowed, many crew members came to CD/TE11B to compare notes, facts, and speculations with him. Junior officer that he was, he was looked to as an expert on the Dylintari by the rest of his crewmates. A bit overcome by it all, he began to think his ears would be pink with embarrassment for the rest of his life.

The Dylintari were very unique when compared to other races the Vlivlarians had dealt with. It seemed amazing that their farming techniques could be so highly advanced when their ship designs were not. Their ships were used exclusively for hauling crops, livestock, and supplies from one settlement hub to another. They had no warships. In fact, their ships showed no weaponry of any kind. Neither did their settlement hubs, whether on planet or moon. In CD/TE11B's eyes, they appeared to be perfectly satisfied, content, and happy within their own system with no worry of what else the universe might contain. All of that was about to change.

CD/TE11B began his watch that morning by reviewing data received while he was off duty. He was concerned when he found that communications had been lost between the central world and the smaller planet. His concern deepened when he discovered how distressed the Dylintari were over this. Evidently, this was an anomaly they had never dealt with before. From the messages he read, they had never lost communications between settlements in their history. After failing to gain a response over a few hours time, the Dylintari sent ships to investigate the smaller planet.

The young engineer keyed for data from the probes near the planet in question to see if he could discover the reason it had gone silent. To his surprise, all the probes had gone off-line. He checked through the ship's reports and found that Probe Operations/Data Retrieval had not been able to bring them back up. They had shifted orbit of several other probes to investigate. CD/TE11B was hoping to see a report from either the Dylintari ships or Vlivlarian probes to explain what was happening before he went off duty. The ships and probes were unable to report anything; they just disappeared. One moment they were there, the next they were gone. He barely slept that night as he reviewed every report for the last two days hoping to find a clue.

When he came on duty the next day, he found that two of the moons had also gone silent. The Dylintari messages showed a growing panic. They were unable to reach so many of their settlements and those which still had communications were filling the airwaves trying to find out what was happening. CD/TE11B and his team worked feverishly to find some explanation in their data. They too came up with nothing! The moons had been sending out reports and messages as usual, then simply stopped. By late afternoon, the third moon went silent.

A ship wide announcement came through on the Communications Deck tech screen. The Ship Commander had called an emergency meeting of the command staff debating whether to break protocol and take the ship in closer. CD/TE11B hoped they would. With the more powerful equipment they had on board ship, they might be able to ascertain the cause of the lost communications. Others in his department were not convinced this would be the best course of action. Vlivlarians always stuck to protocol, but how did one measure the importance of remaining undetected with the possibility of helping a terrified race deal with circumstances that were beyond their comprehension? The whole crew was relieved to hear messages had been sent both to Vlivlary and the Space League of Worlds' Command Central asking for orders or advice. Unfortunately, this only led to more debate and speculation in a situation where time was of the essence.

For the first time in his life, CD/TE11B contemplated breaking protocol. He very much wanted to respond and let the Dylintari know their messages had been received by someone. That there were beings out there who cared about what was happening and wished to help if they could. But he did not. He was Vlivlarian. He could not force himself to go against protocol, no matter how great his personal desire.

CD/TE11B did refuse to leave his post. He could not abandon the Dylintari. He became glued to his techpad. He felt completely helpless knowing that all he could do was watch the messages as they scrolled by. His ears were an ever deepening blue as each message grew more frantic than the last. Gone were all the farming updates. Now the channels were flooded with questions about what was happening and what was being done to find out. Messages from family members searching for loved ones tore at his heart. Communications continued to be sent to the silent settlements, but none were received or answered. No messages were transmitted from those hubs, or even the areas of space near them. More and more ships, both official and personal, were flying all over the system trying to find answers. One by one, each ship would disappear.

Finally, a message from one of the searchers reached his techpad, raising the engineer's hope. Those hopes were dashed when he read what it contained.

"Everything is gone! It is all destroyed! All of our people—" then the message just stopped.

For a moment, it was as if the Dylintari people were holding their breath right along with CD/TE11B. No messages were sent for several heartbeats, as if they waited for the rest of the report to come through. Then messages of terror and distress started scrolling up his techpad's screen so quickly the engineer could barely read them. Suddenly, it went blank.

CD/TE11B's ears shifted between shades of green and blue, showing his confusion and mourning for a people he had never met, yet felt he knew. He was crushed by the final message sent by a Vlivlarian probe before it was destroyed.

"Weapons firing on planet. Origin unknown. Intensity phenomenal. Destruction complete."

He barely noticed when the Ship Commander ordered the triggering of the self-destruct on all remaining probes and the immediate withdrawal from the system. The ship dropped a stealthed, long-range probe as the ship's coordinates were set for a location in the next sector. The Vlivlarians were able to escape the system undetected.

Several weeks later, CD/TE11B was very much surprised to be called to the Ship Commander's staff meeting room. Upon his arrival, he found the Commanders of all units and sections already present.

After acknowledging each of the senior officers, he took the seat indicated at the end opposite the Ship Commander.

"Communications Detection/Translation Engineer 11B, we have called you here today for a most important purpose," the Ship Commander began. "We have received a full and final report from the probe left in the Dylintari system." He paused for a moment, his ears shading to a deep blue before he continued, his voice filled with pain and regret.

"The entire system has been destroyed. There is nothing left on either planet or on any of the three moons. In fact, one moon no longer exists. There is not one ship or probe to be found in the system. Every building, field, and living thing has been completely obliterated."

The junior officer slowly looked around the table, seeing the mourning of each officer present. His own grief became almost unbearable in that moment. He had spent so much time studying their messages and discovering how they lived that he felt he knew the Dylintari. It was almost like a member of his family had been taken from him. Though he had never seen or even spoken to them, they had become part of his very existence.

The Ship Commander gave CD/TE11B a few moments to regain his composure before he spoke again.

"We share your grief over the destruction of such a peaceful and innocent people. The command staff and I sent a request to the High Council on Vlivlary. I have just received their answer."

At his signal, the Communications Commander brought up the following message on the meeting room's tech screen.

"To honor the fallen race of the Dylintari, and so no Vlivlarian or member of the Space League of World shall ever forget their destruction, we decree that a sub-krontomic receiver/transmitter shall henceforth be included in every communications bank in the Space League of Worlds. These will stand, not only as a memorial to a lost people, but also as a vow to do everything within our power to see that a tragedy of this nature and magnitude is never allowed to happen again.

"We wish to acknowledge Communications Detection/Translations Engineer 11B for his contribution in the discovery of sub-krontomic waves and the design of the aforementioned unit. He will henceforth be promoted to Junior SubCommander of the Communications Detection/Translations Engineer division 11. We realize this is small compensation for the grief you suffered over the Dylintari's destruction, but hope that in this position you will be able to help keep a similar tragedy from happening to any other race.

"Protocols have been changed to allow Ship Commanders to use their own discretion when intervening to help a race prior to contact is deemed necessary."

The Ship Commander made his way to Junior Sub-Commander 11's side. The newly minted officer left his chair and came to attention. The Ship Commander attached the new rank emblem to his uniform, and the entire command staff came to their feet and saluted him.

Junior SubCommander 11 raised his hand and gently touched his new emblem, then let his eyes circle the faces around the table before turning to his Ship Commander.

"I am truly humbled by the great honor I have been given. I will do my part, to the best of my small abilities, to see that the Dylintari will NEVER be forgotten. Nor will I ever give up the hope that somehow, someway, at least one of their race escaped and may yet be found."

With that statement, he saluted, turned and exited the room leaving the silent Command Staff behind him.

Evicted!

Becca Lynn Rudder

L et me tell you about my first apartment. It's been several years since I lived there, but I remember it like it was just yesterday. It was just one room, but I thought it was the perfect little home. I had everything I needed: a place to sleep, food to eat. It was rather dark in there—a couple different shades of deep purple—but I didn't mind. It was my favorite place to be. That was a good thing, too; I never went anywhere else.

The first few months I lived there, I have to admit, weren't the most eventful you could imagine. That time was spent settling in to my new home and new everyday routines. The latter included getting used to the quakes that happened every few days or so. Overall, the apartment wasn't that bad, but I sure wished it were in a different neighborhood sometimes. Those quakes always made me jump!

After I finished getting acquainted with my home—about the fifth month I had lived there, I believe—I started gymnastics training. I wasn't very good; I rammed into the wall more often than not. My apartment would bounce when I did that. I don't know why. I kept on tumbling and cart-wheeling—and face-planting—for the remainder of my time there. I did get better as the months went by. At least, I'd like to say so. Nobody told me otherwise.

My apartment was a little crowded with cushions. Not tables and chairs—not even a bed—just cushions. All different shapes and sizes of them, some dark purple like the walls, some even darker, a few maybe a little lighter. They were fine for the occasional rest and relaxation, or maybe stopping for a bite to eat, but I preferred to use them for fighting practice.

Yes, I liked to use the cushions for punching bags—or kicking bags, depending on what self-defense skill I was trying to hone at the time. The apartment jerked and jumped when I did that, too . . . especially when I threw a good jab at the little cushions on the floor towards the back of the room, or made a flying kick into one of the big ones on the ceiling in front. I loved it. You may think I'm strange, maybe even a little crazy, but I did. I loved it!

Another thing I loved about my home was the music coming from outside. Somewhere out there, someone was often singing or humming. The melodies were very soothing and calmed me down when a recent quake or something had me a bit scared. The voice would often talk right outside my room, too, which might have been annoying to some people. I didn't mind, though; I could listen to the voice all the time. It made me happy when I heard it.

A few more months went by, and my one-room apartment started to seem a bit tight. I knew I was outgrowing it and needed to find someplace bigger, but it was where I had always lived. I felt safe there; I didn't really want to leave, even if the quarters were a bit cramped. I could manage just fine still, certainly. It was my home, and I would stay.

Sadly, that philosophy only worked a precious few more weeks before the unthinkable happened—I was being evicted! I couldn't believe it! I was being thrown out of my own home!

I fought to stay as long as I could, but soon I was being forced through the door. Where would I go? I had never been out there before; I didn't know what it was like. I was scared out of my mind, and still they forced me to leave. Inch by inch, I was dragged out, head first, into the great unknown.

If that wasn't enough, as they were pulling me out, it started getting very bright. I had never seen brightness like that before, and after they finished getting me out, it was even worse. Light shone so brightly all around me that, for a few minutes, I couldn't even see!

When I finally regained my sight in all that light, I saw the strangest thing I had ever seen. Some creature was holding me in its thin paws, studying me. I studied it in return, between frightened sobs. First, I saw its face—it being right over mine—and it was like the face of a . . . ferret, I believe my friend Cat calls it. In fact, she says that its whole head and much of its body is like an oversized one of these ferret creatures, even having a tail! I only saw its face and head then, however, and just knew that they were a creamy color with some dark brown on its face and the top of its ears and head, looking to continue on back from the latter.

The ferret-like creature looked up at something behind my head. "Nurse Jonyt," it said, holding me out in front of it carefully.

"Yes, Dr. Timnes," another voice replied, and suddenly I was taken from paws to arms by its owner, who I decided must be this Nurse Jonyt that Ferret-face—well, I mean, Dr. Timnes—had addressed.

After detaching me from my home, Nurse Jonyt helped me get cleaned up and refreshed from the whole ordeal, and wrapped me in a blanket so that I wouldn't get too cold in the admittedly frigid room I was in. I looked around as she did all this, trying to take in the room, but it was confusing. It was easy to see that it was very clean, but there were many strange metal objects all over the place that really frightened me. So I looked at Nurse Jonyt instead.

Her face and head looked nothing like those of Dr. Timnes. She seemed more like a human—like Cat—only with lavender-blue skin, like I could see that my own hands were as I squirmed around a bit, only hers was a little darker. Short, pearly-white hair swooped outward from beneath the blue nurses' cap she wore atop her head, and violet eyes shone down at me as well as a gentle smile while she worked.

Soon Nurse Jonyt finished tidying me up and handed me back to Dr. Timnes. He looked at me with an odd expression on his face—which I have come to know is as close to a smile as a ferret's face can form—then carried me a little ways and held me out to someone else. She had a lighter lavender-blue skin color like I did, with long pearly-white hair flowing down over her shoulders. "Here is your baby girl, Sylinta," Dr. Timnes said as the woman took me into her arms.

"My little Zupani," she whispered as she held me close, bright purple eyes sparkling as she looked down at me.

And I knew that voice! That was the voice outside my apartment, that had talked to me and sung to me all the months I lived there! I didn't cry anymore; I felt safe. I knew that she loved me and would take care of me. I wasn't worried now that my mother had me wrapped in her arms.

Why do you look so surprised? *Your* mother was the first apartment *you* had, and you would have had to have been evicted from her to be here listening to me, wouldn't you?

The Omega Mission

Douglas Rudder

Major Buck Gresham stared out the side window of the troop compartment of the helicopter, watching the rugged terrain rush by below, oblivious to the conversation around him. The evening sun rode low on the horizon, casting deep shadows across the craggy landscape that matched the darkness of the Major's mood. The helicopter was running in stealth mode, low and silent, with a second bird tailing it transporting the rest of his commando team.

Their target, an old weapons manufacturing plant, had been abandoned after the war. The plant's remote location had supposedly been a carefully guarded secret at the height of the conflict. Devastating enemy air strikes had put that notion to rest, as well as the productivity of the plant. Still, most of the complex remained intact enough to provide a defensible hideaway for a determined group of terrorists.

And somewhere in those ruins they held a hostage: a scared, defenseless little girl.

The abducted girl was the daughter of Ambassador Jalen Wistrom from Poltaris, a former Earth colony that was now part of the Pegasus Sector Coalition. Wistrom represented the PSC delegation sent to negotiate a mutual defense treaty against the growing aggression of the Ghalnaar Dynasty, after two outer rim worlds had fallen to the Ghalnaari fleet. A small and violent faction within the PSC opposed the treaty and vowed to disrupt the conference.

The renegades contracted with a terrorist group known as the Omega Network to kidnap Wistrom's daughter, Arianna. Their attack had been swift and bloody, leaving much of the Poltari security force and a squad of U.S. Marines dead in its wake. Within hours, they had issued an ultimatum: unless the Coalition pulled out of the negotiations, the girl would be killed as an object lesson to the Coalition leaders.

Gresham's mission parameters were clear: infiltrate the enemy stronghold, locate and secure Arianna Wistrom, and bring her back alive.

A night raid against the Omega Network cell would be challenging, but Gresham and his unit had gone up against them before. He knew their tactics and understood their methods. Omega leaders were cold, calculating, and vicious. Omega troops were brutal. They inflicted indiscriminate death and destruction to wreak havoc and paralyze their victims with fear. Human life meant nothing to them, except as a means to gain the upper hand as hostages or shields, or to provide profits, or as leverage to attain their goals. Yes, he had fought them before, had seen their grisly handiwork first hand.

Only this time they had an innocent ten-year-old child as their pawn—a child the same age as his own son, Bobby.

Just imagining Bobby in the hands of a band of stone-cold killers drove a dagger through his heart, eliciting a pang of empathy for the desperation the ambassador and his wife must be feeling. The muscles in his jaws tightened. He promised himself silently that his team would find the ambassador's daughter and return her to her family, alive and safe.

Gresham inhaled deeply and released his breath slowly. He needed to keep his emotions in check. Not bottled up completely, but redirected to the task at hand. A heartless soldier was just as dangerous as a hyper-emotional one. Finding the right mix of objectivity and passion was key. He refused to be an automaton, but he also could not let emotions make him reckless.

That had already happened to him once recently. In one unguarded moment, he made a crucial mistake that led to a confrontation with his son.

Memories of that night flooded over him as he stared out into the deepening twilight.

Eight months before, his wife, Janet, had been killed in a hit-and-run car accident. Police found the other car, which had been reported stolen earlier in the day, abandoned a few miles down the road. Beer bottles littered the floorboards, but no other sign of the driver remained. Some joy-rider out for a good time had taken the life of the woman he loved—and left his son without a mother.

The first few weeks were rough as he dealt with both his son's grief and his own. Then he was called away on a mission and had to figure out how to take care of

Bobby while he was gone. Their closest family lived half a continent away. Gresham left Bobby with some friends for the ten days he was deployed. But that was not a long-term solution.

In the end, he reluctantly listened to the higher ups and did something he thought he would never do: he hired a nanny. The idea had always seemed a little ostentatious to him, but he was left with little choice. HQ even did the leg-work for him and recommended a woman the New York office had used before in similar circumstances. She would be part-time and live in her own apartment, but would stay with Bobby whenever the Major had to be away. That she was willing to fly to Texas on short notice to take the position spoke to her passion for the role.

Her name was Ann Chambers. She was in her early thirties, with a soft voice and an endearing Brooklyn accent, and usually wore her dark hair in a ponytail. Gresham recognized early on that her almost perky demeanor was tailored to make Bobby feel more at ease with her. Her eyes held a watchful intelligence that went beyond the lighthearted persona she projected.

Bobby, of course, did not like the idea one bit. Their initial meeting at Gresham's house was tense for a while, but ended as well as could be expected. Bobby still seemed uncertain, but was willing to give it a try.

Ann had brushed off Gresham's apology for his son's reluctance. "Don't worry about it, Major. He'll come around. I haven't lost one yet." Her eyes clouded a little. "Bobby has lost a parent, just like the other children I've taken care of. What's worse for these kids is that when their remaining parent is deployed, they never know if that parent is going to come home again."

"Thank you for understanding, Miss Chambers," Gresham answered. "It's quite a job you have taken on, caring for kids who have lost so much."

"It's not a job, Major. It's a mission." She gave him a gentle smile. "And my name is Ann, not Miss Chambers."

"Then my name is Buck, not Major."

"All right, Buck. I'll be here with Bobby whenever you are away. Here," she said, handing him a piece of paper. "This is my address and cell phone number. Just give me a call if you need me to come over for any reason."

To his great relief Bobby had eventually warmed to her, and they got along pretty well when Gresham was away. Over time, Ann began spending more time with the two of them, sometimes staying for a while after putting Bobby to bed to just sit and chat. Ann was pleasant company and easy to talk to.

Then it happened. The night before he left for his current mission, Ann had spent the evening with him, and their conversation had gone well into the night.

When the time came, he walked her to the door. "Good night, Ann. I'll see you in the morning. I have to head out early."

"Good night, Buck," Ann replied. "I know you can't talk about your mission, but . . ." She looked flustered for a second, and then took both of his hands in hers. "Please be careful," she whispered, and kissed him on the cheek.

She lingered near, her cheek not quite touching his. The smell of her hair, of her perfume, filled his senses. They stood there silently for a moment, and then he leaned down and kissed her.

"NO!" Bobby's voice exploded behind him.

He jerked free from Ann like she was a livewire and spun around to face his son. The despair in Bobby's expression tore at his heart.

Ann touched his arm. "Buck, I didn't know . . . I didn't mean for him to see . . ." her voice trailed off uncertainly.

"It's not your fault," he assured her. "I'll take care of it."

She nodded. "Maybe I'd better go. Good night, Buck."

After she left, he closed the door and motioned Bobby over to the couch. "Come here, son. I guess we need to talk, don't we?"

Bobby came over and sat down, directing his sullen stare at the coffee table. "She's not Mom," he said as his father started to sit down beside him.

Gresham hesitated mid-motion. "You're right. She's not," he answered, continuing the rest of the way down.

His son brought his eyes up to meet his, then looked away again. "Don't you love Mom anymore?"

A hollowness settled in his chest, a sense of loss that he hadn't felt since the day Janet died. "I will always love your mother, Bobby," he said, struggling to keep his voice from breaking. "Look at me, son." He reached out and gently turned his son's face toward him. "*Look* at me. I'm not in love with Ann. Maybe someday I'll fall in love again; I don't know. But it won't be any time soon."

"Then why did you kiss her?"

Gresham didn't really have a good answer for that one. It puzzled him too. He had meant what he said, yet he had still kissed Ann. He hadn't seen that coming.

He put his arm around Bobby, and his son leaned against his chest. They sat there holding each other, until Bobby finally drifted off to sleep.

Leaving his son behind the next morning without really resolving anything had been difficult. Bobby was not thrilled with Ann coming over, but he did behave himself pretty well and did not make a scene. For her part, Ann took it in stride and assured Gresham that they would be fine while he was away. Still, he could not shake his misgivings as he hugged Bobby and departed for the base. With Janet gone, his son needed him now more than ever.

With an effort, Gresham brought his attention back to the present. Maybe after this mission, he would turn the unit over to Dan and ask for a desk job. But for now, distractions would only hurt the mission, and he could not let that happen—not with a little girl's life hanging in the balance.

Shifting in his seat, he wiggled his shoulders a little to resettle his combat gear more comfortably. He lifted his tablet and brought up the schematics of the complex again. Five flashing red dots marked areas that Intelligence tagged as the most likely places to hold a prisoner. A scattering of yellow dots marked secondary locations. He and his second-in-command, Captain Dan Quintaine, had spent long hours mapping out scenarios and had divided the list into sets of four, in order of priority, pursuant to sign-off by the higher ups. If anyone could spot a hole in the plan, it would be Dan. His eye for detail and almost uncanny ability to analyze each option and visualize the possible endpoints made him an invaluable asset.

Glancing across the troop compartment, Gresham noted that Dan had his own tablet out, going over some notes with his teammate—and wife—Karen. Some higher ups looked down on members of a combat team getting married, but Gresham was not about to break up that pairing. They worked so smoothly together it was like they were inside each other's minds.

Beside them sat bulky Percy Pendleton, giving his compact but powerful Aries assault rifle a final check—and taking up more than his share of the compartment. Gresham had to resist the temptation to call him Hoss after one of his favorite old vid archive Western characters. Having seen Pendleton upend the last guy who called him that, it seemed the better part of valor to keep it to himself.

The Quintaines and Pendleton made up Bravo Team. Charlie Team, under the leadership of Lieutenant Rachel Higashi, and Delta Team, led by Sergeant Bruno Cavallo, rode in the second helicopter.

Gresham himself headed up Alpha Team. The other members of his team, DeAuntae Britt and Valeria Alvarez, were currently engaged in their usual schoolyard trash talking.

"You do realize," Alvarez was saying, "those shades are going to be useless when we hit the ground, don't you?"

Britt's sleek wrap sunglasses did look out of place in the gathering dusk. Not that it deterred him any. "True," he said, leaning back and lacing his fingers behind his head. "But nothin' says I can't look good while we ride."

Alvarez made a gagging sound. She waved a hand over his chest. "And what's with all those pouches? That one's not even regulation!"

"More ammo, pictures of my girl. Oh, and cheese and crackers in case I get hungry between firefights."

Britt was the unit's "geardo," who regularly added extra, seemingly unnecessary pieces and parts to his gear. It never ceased to amaze his teammates how often he pulled something unexpectedly useful out of one of those pouches at the most relevant moments.

"Mm, hmm." Alvarez wasn't through with him yet. "What is that?" she asked, peering at one of his side pouches. "Is that a tiny *teddy bear?*"

"Don't touch it," He warned. He slapped her hand as she reached for it. "Don't touch my teddy bear."

The rest of the compartment went silent, except for the muted whooshing of helicopter blades.

Britt's eyes swept over the others self-consciously, as if just realizing how that sounded. "It's not for me," he insisted. "It's for the kid."

Alvarez lifted an eyebrow in one of her patented "oh, really?" looks.

Britt spread his hands, exasperated. "What? She's going through some scary stuff. I thought it might make her feel better on the way home."

"That's sweet."

"Knock it off," Britt huffed.

"No," Alvarez smiled. "I mean it. That really is sweet, you big tough softy."

Gresham caught Dan's eye and exchanged grins. Then he sobered. Britt was right; the little girl was alone and afraid.

Dan seemed to pick up on his thoughts. "We'll get her out, Chief."

"You got that right," Britt agreed.

Alvarez leaned forward to see around Britt. "Whatever it takes, Chief."

"I know we will," he answered. "And don't call me Chief."

*   *   *   *

The helicopters set down behind a ridge about two kilometers out from the complex. Stars glittered in the night sky, but the moon had not yet ascended. Gresham and Dan Quintaine climbed to the top of the ridge and knelt behind a rocky outcropping to survey the shadowed landscape between them and the ruins of the manufacturing plant. None of the out-buildings or grounds around the main building showed any lights. The lighting in the main complex itself appeared sparse, but adequate for the terrorists' purpose.

"Looks like they got the generators up and running," Dan commented. "I'd guess that they had to string temporary lighting inside because of damage to the main lines."

"Agreed." Gresham gestured toward the far right side of the building. "The east side is almost totally dark. It seems to have taken the brunt of the bombing during the war."

"That's where your team is going in, isn't it?"

Gresham slid down behind the outcropping and brought up his tablet display. He pointed at the screen. "Right here. Our first target is a bit farther in, probably beyond the damaged area. We should still be good to go."

Dan nodded absently. He looked thoughtful as he gazed at the display. "I still think that pressure chamber should be rated higher than some of our other target zones."

"You could be right. Intelligence had it rated as third on the list for your team, right?"

"Yes."

Gresham rubbed his jaw. "Let's stick to the plan for

the red targets. But if you want to shift to the pressure chamber as your secondary goal, you're free to do so. Use your best judgment."

"Thanks, Chief."

"We'd better get rolling." Gresham shut down his tablet and tucked it back in its pouch. "We'll maintain radio silence as long as we can and keep our HUDs inactive until the girl is found. Our encryption should be solid, but I don't want to chance the Omegas picking up our signals inside their compound while we're still searching."

They slipped their helmets back on and made their way back down the slope to rejoin the others. After final instructions had been given and gear checked one last time, they headed out.

The commandos split into four groups of three and fanned out, each team taking a different route to the target zone, making use of the rough terrain, shrubbery, battle debris, and out-buildings to hide their approach. Each commando wore a poncho over their combat gear containing a coolant system to mask their heat signatures.

Alpha Team's progress had been slow but uneventful, which suited Gresham just fine. They were still comfortably within their allotted time frame. He resisted the urge to switch on his HUD and check the progress of the other teams. Now they crouched behind an equipment shed, just a few meters from the main building.

Unfortunately, an Omega Network sentry stood guard between them and their intended ingress point.

Alvarez raised her hand, and then tapped the hilt of the knife strapped to her boot. Gresham could not see her face behind her helmet visor in the darkness, but he could imagine her questioning look.

He considered for a moment, then waved her off. As much as he hated to leave an enemy at their back, he did not want to take the chance of alerting the Omegas to their presence this early in the game. The sentry was not wearing a helmet, but he did have a headset on. Undoubtedly he was to report in at regular intervals.

Ideally, when they called the helicopters in for pick-up, their gunners would lay down cover fire and eliminate the outside sentries before the commandos exited the building. Of course, that required the sentries to play nice and remain outside after the alarm went out, but if they didn't, the commandos were more than ready to handle them when the time came.

Britt patted his shoulder and pointed toward a gap in the east wall where a bomb had laid waste to the upper floors. The fissure reached almost to ground level, well within climbing distance.

Gresham nodded and glanced back at the sentry. The guard fiddled with something on his belt, then lifted a pair of night-vision binoculars to his eyes and began scanning the terrain outside. Gresham signaled the other two and silently headed for the break in the wall.

They scrambled up the rubble. When they reached the breach, Alvarez stopped them before climbing through. She slowly ran her hand above a thin wire that was strung across the opening, a few inches from the base. Hoisting herself up a little higher, she inspected the opening and the floor beyond it. Finally, she motioned that the room below was clear of traps and they could go over the tripwire safely.

Once inside, they doffed their ponchos and stuffed them behind a fallen, twisted girder. A wisp of smoke wafted up as the cooling systems burned themselves out. No use leaving free tech behind for any Omega survivors to pick up.

Britt slapped Alvarez on the back. "Good eye spotting that tripwire, Super Scout."

"Thanks, Teddy Bear Man."

Britt groaned. "Aw, man. You aren't ever gonna let that go, are you?"

"Nope," she responded. "It's still got a lot of mileage left in it."

"All right, youngsters," Gresham cut in. "We need to find a way through and we need to find it fast. The clock is ticking."

Pulling out his flashlight, he aimed it at the floor and flicked it on. "Shine your lights low," he cautioned Britt and Alvarez. "We don't want to draw the attention of unfriendly eyes."

They nodded their acknowledgement and spread out, winding through the wreckage in search of an opening to the corridor that would lead to their first objective: a secure storage room, not too far from their present location.

Gresham picked his way through the ruins toward the inner wall. It looked worse on the inside than it had from the ridge earlier. The floors above had collapsed inward, burying whatever doors might have given them access to inner corridors. Maybe he should have let Alvarez take that sentry outside and come in through that entrance.

He shook his head. No use second-guessing himself; it was the right decision. The logic still tracked. They just needed to find an alternate path forward.

A flicker of a flashlight beam caught the edge of his

helmet visor. He swung around to face the source, his Aries assault rifle at the ready. Britt waved at him, and then redirected his flashlight past him toward Alvarez to get her attention as well. Gresham hurried over, arriving just ahead of Alvarez.

Once again, Britt had come through.

As they approached, Britt grinned and slapped the ladder rising up beside him. "So, what do you think of DeAuntae Britt's tunnel in the sky?"

"It's unconventional," Gresham commented dryly, shining his flashlight up to where the ladder attached to an entry port in the metal tube that hung suspended from the ceiling. It appeared to be about four meters above the floor, and maybe a couple out from the wall. "But it might do the trick. Alvarez?"

The young scout nodded thoughtfully. "I think so." She lifted her own flashlight, "I'm going to light it up again for a second."

"Go ahead, but not too long."

"Yes, Major." She quickly ran her beam along the tube to where it intersected with the inner wall. "Notice how it follows the outer wall and parallels the machinery up there. I'd guess it functions as a maintenance crawl-way. It appears to pass through the side wall into the next room. There's a good chance if we crawl through we'll find another ladder on the other side."

"That's my thinking as well," Gresham agreed.

Alvarez slung her rifle over her shoulder and shinnied up the ladder, while Britt and Gresham covered her from below. After she disappeared into the crawlway, Britt followed her up and in, then swung around to cover Gresham's ascent.

The diffused glow of Alvarez' light greeted him at the top. As he braced his hands and started to lift himself through the opening, he heard Alvarez give a muffled shout. Britt's head snapped toward him and the soldier's foot shot out in a wild kick, catching Gresham hard in the sternum.

Gresham grunted as the impact of Britt's boot knocked him off the ladder. The shock of the kick and sensation of falling flared in the pit of his stomach, and his arms and legs flailed as he plummeted.

He was still in mid-air when the crawlway exploded.

* * * *

A moaning sound penetrated the haze in Gresham's mind, barely audible over the throbbing in his skull and ringing in his ears. He forced his eyes open as another moan escaped his lips. His whole body ached, and he was sprawled at an odd angle, judging by the skewed look of the darkened environment around him.

He started to push himself upright, then gasped as a sharp pain shot through his left side, jolting him fully awake. Gingerly, he probed his ribcage with his fingers and winced. A couple of ribs were at least deeply bruised, if not cracked. It could be worse; that explosion could have ripped him apart.

The explosion.

He rolled awkwardly off the pile of rubble and struggled to his feet, fingers frantically clawing at his gear until they closed on his flashlight. He flicked the switch, illuminating the scene before him.

What was left of the crawlway jutted out from the wall above. The rest of the tube lay in a mangled, jumbled mess on the floor below. Dust was still settling, which meant he had only been out for a few moments. He yanked his first aid kit from its pouch and stumbled over to the broken crawlway. In the distance, he could hear shouts and booted feet running down a corridor. He picked up his pace, shoving debris aside in an effort to reach his team before the Omega guards arrived.

Alvarez and Britt were dead. The sight of his fallen teammates wrenched at his insides. He knelt beside them and pounded his fist against the remains of the tube. If Alvarez hadn't shouted her warning, if Britt hadn't kicked him off the ladder, he would have died with them. They deserved better than this.

Another shout sounded beyond the wall. Gresham's hand went to his holster; the Omegas could be on him any minute. His brows furrowed. Why weren't they here already? Surely they would investigate the explosion. He paused and listened. Then he understood.

He activated his helmet comm. "This is Alpha Leader. We hit a booby trap. They know we're here."

Dan's voice responded first, "Casualties?"

"Two," Gresham answered, his throat tight. He swallowed hard, then went on, "I hear a lot of enemy activity, all moving inward from my position."

"Understood. Our primary target came up dry; Bravo is closing on secondary target."

"Delta Leader here," Bruno Cavallo's voice broke in. "Enemy troops are moving away from us as well, toward the inner complex."

Gresham nodded to himself. "Just watch yourselves. They'll most likely establish a perimeter to keep us out. Don't assume they've all left your area."

The Omega movements narrowed it down to either

Bravo Team or Charlie Team having the best chance to locate the girl, and he would bet dollars to donuts on Dan Quintaine's hunch about that pressure chamber.

Now he just had to get moving himself—leaving Britt and Alvarez behind.

It didn't feel right to just leave them, but the best thing he could do for them now was complete their mission, to bring Arianna Wistrom home. He stood up, looking one last time at his fallen companions. His flashlight beam swept across something small and fuzzy.

There, dangling from its pouch, appearing none the worse for wear except for a singed ear, was Britt's teddy bear.

Reaching down, he gently scooped up the teddy bear and tucked it in the side of his belt, a fresh sense of determination welling up inside him. There was one more thing he could do for his friends.

The stub of the crawlway still seemed like his best bet for getting through to the other side. He retrieved the ladder and lifted it up to the tube, hooking it over a jagged edge where the tube had torn away. After climbing into the crawlway, he grasped the ladder and swung it away from the opening, sending it clattering to the floor. No use leaving evidence of his passage. With luck, the inevitable searchers would assume the whole team had been caught in the blast.

He did not encounter any more traps as he silently passed through the crawlway. The access port on the other side showed a faint light. He approached it carefully and peeked through into what appeared to be another large manufacturing area. From his vantage point, the room appeared empty of guards, but an open door at his far right showed a lighted corridor.

Eschewing the rungs, he slid down the ladder, quickly and silently. As he hefted his rifle and started toward the door, gunfire erupted in the distance, deeper inside the complex. He broke into a run, keeping his body low in case he wasn't as alone as it seemed.

His comm crackled to life. "Bravo is road runner!" Dan's voice shouted. "Repeat, Bravo is road runner!"

Gresham grinned. Dan had called it. "All teams, converge and protect." He switched his comm channel to signal the helicopters. "Porter, the hostage is secured and we are outbound! Get those birds in the air. Cover and watch for pickup at Bravo One egress point."

"Roger, Alpha Leader."

Gresham activated his heads-up display. An overlay of the complex schematics appeared, with small green dots representing the rest of his squad flashing on the display. Charlie Team had hooked up with Bravo already, while Delta was drifting back to the perimeter to establish an exit corridor. Gresham examined the schematics to determine his best route to the others, then switched the display back off. Their encryption was good, but that didn't mean the Omega Network could not break it given enough time.

He spotted a hallway just up ahead and put on an adrenaline-infused burst of speed. If he hurried, he still had time to connect with Delta and secure their exit vector before Bravo arrived with the girl. He raced around the corner into the side passage.

And abruptly skidded to a halt. He froze, trying to make sense of the scene before him.

"Ann?"

"Hello, Buck. Nice to see you again." Ann Chambers stood in the middle of the corridor, clad in black Omega Network combat fatigues. Bobby stood next to her, looking none too happy—with good reason: Ann's left arm was around his shoulders; her right hand held a snub-nosed Beretta submachine gun against his head.

Instinctively, Gresham brought up his assault rifle, his grip tightening.

Ann cocked her head and raised her right elbow, pressing her weapon more firmly against Bobby's head, eliciting a grunt from him. "Ah, ah," she said. "This SMG is loaded with armor-piercing rounds. Imagine the awful things they will do to Bobby's skull if you don't lower your weapon."

Slowly, Gresham lowered the barrel to point at the floor, heart hammering in his chest. He shifted his rifle to his left hand and with his right reached up and popped open his helmet visor.

"Good," Ann said evenly. "Now, set your rifle on the floor and slide it over to me. Then, using your left hand, do the same with your sidearm.

She smiled at him. "By the way, it was kind of you to break radio silence so I could pinpoint your location and reunite you with your son."

He ignored her and turned his gaze to Bobby. "Are you all right, son?"

"Yeah," Bobby answered, glowering sidewise at Ann past the weapon pressed against his skull. "But I don't think I want her to be my nanny anymore."

Ann laughed. "You know, I like Bobby, I really do."

Her eyes hardened. "It's too bad I'm going to have to kill him unless you do *exactly* as I say."

Gresham didn't move. "What is it that you want?" he asked, although he already knew the answer. He had to buy time to gather his wits, to settle his swirling thoughts.

"First, I want you to do as I said and slide your weapons over here. Then I want you to call your unit and tell them to surrender. If you want, just have one of them deliver the ambassador's daughter back to us and the rest can leave." She looked him square in the eye. "After we have the girl, you and Bobby can go too."

He had to hand it to her. She was a pretty good straight-faced liar. But something in her posture, like a cobra ready to strike, and the trace of venom in her eyes told him that he and his son were never going to leave there alive.

"Why, Ann? Why are you doing this?"

"My name's not Ann; it's Jasmine. Sweet little Ann died about a month before your wife did." She gave a casual shrug. "I needed to borrow her identity for a while, so one thing led to another, and here we are."

His eyes narrowed. "So you took advantage of my wife's death to . . ." His voice trailed off as the true horror of the situation hit him right in the gut.

Jasmine gave him a faint, evil smile. "That's right, Buck. Janet's death wasn't an accident. This plan has been in the works for almost a year now. We knew your unit would be the one called in to rescue the girl. After all, you are the best."

She pulled her gun away from Bobby's head and waved it in his direction. "Oh, the irony of it all. You see, *I* was the other driver. That's right, Buck. I killed your wife, I babysat your son—and I made you fall for me."

A cold rage chilled his heart. He wanted to lash out, to rip the throat from that vile, gloating, murderous creature. Peripherally, he saw Bobby standing next to her, his own eyes filled with terror, anger, and hopelessness. He knew she was trying to goad him, to keep him off balance, to manipulate him. He couldn't let that happen. This had to end.

Explosions sounded outside, joining the staccato of automatic-weapons fire inside, as the helicopters began pounding the Omega sentry positions with rocket salvos.

Jasmine twitched at the sound and glared at Gresham. "Time's up, Buck. Slide your weapon over here *now.*"

"Fine," he bit out. "Here." With a powerful, back-handed sweep of his left arm, he sent his rifle skittering across the floor—right at Jasmine's feet—while his right hand went for his sidearm.

She deftly skipped aside away from Bobby and opened fire.

Armor-piercing rounds ripped through his combat armor, searing into his chest and torso before he even cleared leather. With a cry of agony and desperation, he reeled backward, firing round after round. He had the grim satisfaction of seeing Jasmine jerk repeatedly as his shots found their mark.

The scene took on a surreal aspect as he watched her collapse, even as he fell. Then he found himself lying on his back staring at the ceiling, his vision swimming. He lay there, gasping for air. His efforts were futile; what little breathing he could achieve was ragged and shallow. A burning, excruciating pain wracked his body, and he knew the wetness streaming down his sides and pooling in his combat armor was not just sweat.

"Dad!" Bobby's voice sounded hollow in his ears. He heard his son running toward him.

"Bobby," he whispered. Fighting the urge to pass out, he used his chin to turn on his comm. "Alpha Leader is down."

Dan Quintaine's voice came back almost immediately, accentuated by gunfire in the background. "Is it bad?"

"It's bad. Dan, Bobby's here."

There was a pause. "Say again?"

"Bobby's here," Gresham answered, struggling to get out every word. "Ann . . . was Omega." He gasped again, then said hoarsely, "Save Bobby."

"We're on our way." Gresham could hear the steel in Dan's voice.

Bobby dropped to his knees beside him, hands hovering over his father's chest, afraid to touch him. Gresham could see the terror in his wide eyes as he stared, transfixed, at his father's torn body. It was evident his son was on the verge of shock.

"Son," Gresham rasped. "Look at me." He held his son's gaze and tried to project a calmness he did not feel. "Dan's coming."

"Dan?" Bobby blinked and seemed to relax just a little. "Uncle Dan's coming?"

"Yes."

His son nodded, as if to reassure himself. "It'll be all right, Dad. Uncle Dan will save us. He'll save us."

Gresham tried to lift his hand, but only succeeded in moving his fingers. Bobby must've noticed the motion, because he reached down and took his father's hand, clasping it to his chest.

They waited silently, Bobby hugging his father's

hand and clearly trying to put on a brave face for his dad, Gresham straining to breathe, to stay alive for his son.

Footsteps came rushing down the hall. Bobby's head snapped up in fear, then his eyes brightened. "Uncle Dan! Aunt Karen! Hurry! Dad's hurt!"

Dan stepped into Gresham's view, putting a hand on Bobby's shoulder and glancing over at Jasmine. He shook his head and removed his helmet. "Bobby, I need some room to take a look at your dad. Why don't you go over there with Karen?"

With obvious reluctance, Bobby softly set his father's hand down and moved away.

"Aw, Chief," Dan said softly as he examined Gresham. "What did she do to you?"

Another explosion shook the building. Dan leaned over Gresham to keep dust from falling in his wounds. He looked over at Karen. "Get Bobby out of here. Now."

"No!" Bobby cried. "We can't leave without Dad!"

Gresham heard Karen's soothing voice, "Come on, Bobby. Dan's with your dad."

"Uncle Dan will bring Dad too, right?" Gresham heard his son ask as they headed off at a trot. Karen's soft response was too low for Gresham to hear.

Dan knelt beside Gresham, mouth twisted with emotion, and laid a hand on his CO's arm. "I can't move you, Buck. There's too much damage."

"I know," Gresham mouthed. He coughed as he tried to draw a breath. His son, his poor son. "Bobby?"

"Karen and I will take care of him," Dan promised. "Don't worry."

Gresham nodded, his energy almost gone. His brow furrowed. There was something else chasing around in his head, something else he needed Dan to do. He tried to concentrate, to hold onto that thought. "Left . . . hip," he croaked.

A confused look passed over Dan's face, then the skin around his eyes tightened. He leaned across Gresham and gently plucked Britt's teddy bear from Gresham's belt. "For the girl?"

Gresham nodded. Then, wheezing with the effort, he told his friend, "Go."

Dan rose to his feet. He looked at the toy in his hand, then back down at Gresham. Bowing his head, he put his helmet back on and left.

The corridor grew quiet. The sounds in the distance became indistinct as Gresham's senses faded. He lay there alone, sightless eyes facing the ceiling. The pain was gone. Only numbness remained.

Lord, he prayed, *watch over Bobby. Please.*

He waited in the shadows of a life nearly spent, willing himself to draw in air for just a little bit longer.

Finally, Dan's voice crackled in his headset, "The kids are on board, Chief. We're lifting off. The kids are safe. Chief?"

Lacking the strength to answer, he closed his eyes. Bobby was safe. Arianna Wistrom was safe. His last mission was complete.

As his life ebbed into darkness, he felt a tear trickle across his temple.

Goodbye, son. I love you.

About the Authors

C. K. Deatherage earned her B.A. and M.A. from Southern Illinois University at Edwardsville in English and her Ph.D. from Purdue University in Old and Middle English Language and Literature. Her previous publications include *Waysmeet: Poems and Tales of Fantasy and Wonder*, "Niall MacDonaugh and the Leipreachan" in *The RudderHaven Science Fiction and Fantasy Anthology I*, "Final Entry" in *Star Trek: Strange New Worlds V*, and various poems in anthologies and journals. She won the 2013 Poet of the Year and the 2013 Vardis Fisher Award for Most Humorous Piece by the Idaho Writers League. She currently resides in Idaho with her husband, two kids, two large dogs, and four cats—and an occasional very temporary field mouse.

Becca Lynn Rudder is teen-aged girl with a dream of writing a story—and actually finishing one, finally. She is the daughter of Douglas and Sheri Rudder, both of which are also *RudderHaven* authors. They, as well as other members of her family, helped her with the polishing phases of her story. She knows that she couldn't have finished it without their help. Becca lives in southern Illinois with her parents and their dog, Shadow Star. She enjoys MMOs and PC games, movies and TV shows (especially older ones), reading, and just plain talking. She likes Barbies and Princesses—and *really* likes super-heroes, Star Trek/Star Wars, and Lord of the Rings as well.

Douglas Rudder is a St. Louis area science fiction and fantasy author. He and his brother, Jonathan, are co-publishers and Managing Editors for RudderHaven. He currently resides in southern Illinois, where he often battles Orcs, Aliens, and Super-Villains with his wife and daughter. An avid reader of science fiction and fantasy since childhood, Doug's first book, *Tolkien: Roncevaux, Ethandune, and Middle-earth*, is a work of literary criticism. He is also an author and editor for *The RudderHaven Science Fiction and Fantasy Anthology* series. Current creative endeavors include three novels in various stages of mayhem and several short stories for upcoming anthologies.

Jonathan Rudder graduated with a B.A. in English from Southern Illinois University at Edwardsville and an M.F.A. in Creative Writing from Full Sail University in Winter Park, FL. He and his brother, Douglas, are co-publishers and Managing Editors of RudderHaven, based in Granite City, IL. Inspired at an early age by the works of J.R.R. Tolkien and C.S. Lewis, Jonathan became an avid reader—and later writer—of fantasy and science fiction. He served for almost nine years as the copyeditor, writer, and official Tolkien lore-expert for the award-winning MMO The Lord of the Rings Online™ by Time Warner/Turbine Inc, finishing his career there as a content designer. Currently, Jonathan dedicates most of his time to his family, RudderHaven, and teaching in the fifth highest rated game design degree program in the world, located at Becker College, Worcester, MA.

Sheri Lynn Rudder, a fortunate stay at home wife and mother, grew up in rural, southeast Iowa. Thanks to her mother and grandfather, she learned at an early age that the best place to find adventures was in books. Twenty-six years ago, when she married her knight-in-shining-armour (known to most as Douglas) she was introduced to the wonderful worlds of sci-fi and fantasy, mainly through the writings of JRR Tolkien, Michael Stackpole, and Timothy Zahn. Now, with her husband's encouragement and the quick-clicking editing pen of her teenaged daughter, she is trying her hand at sharing her adventures with you.

RudderHaven Spotlight

The Milhavior Chronicles by Jonathan M. Rudder:

Sharamitaro – *Destiny beckons, but cold hearts cannot hear . . .* Brendys, the simple son of a Horsemaster, finds himself the inheritor of a great token of power and a destiny of which he wants no part . . . that of the Bearer of the Flame, prophesied harbinger of the Heir of Ascon, High King of Milhavior. Plagued by a curse, evil follows Brendys from his home in the small country of Shalkan to Gildea, a nation besieged by a dark power. There, Brendys must face his destiny and the shadows which threaten to consume him or begin a journey through darkness which could cause him to lose all he holds dear.

The Road to Elekar – *There is no Darkness that Light cannot pierce, no Death that Life cannot overcome . . . or is there?* Brendys of Shalkan thought his adventures were over. He had found love and joy, but his past will not stay dead. A curse placed upon him by a drunken stablehand awakens, threatening to destroy all he loves, drawing him into a Shadow which could spell the doom of Milhavior. His only hope is to use the Sword of the Dawn to slay the Sorcerer responsible for the curse . . . a feat he cannot accomplish unless he accepts his Destiny as the Bearer of the Flame.

A Howl on the Wind – *A call has been answered, but destiny is not what it seems . . .* Brendys of Shalkan was destined to become the Bearer of the Flame, wielder of Denasdervien, the Living Flame, Sword of the Dawn. He was ordained to light the way for the Return of Ascon's Heir to the High Throne of Milhavior. He never dreamed that he would have to be the guide and protector of the Heir himself as the Wolves of Machaelon are unleashed against him.

The Winds of a Rising Storm – *The calm before the Storm has broken . . .* Brendys of Shalkan believed that a time of peace had come to him. The agents of Machaelon had not risen up against him or his family in nearly two years, but not all was as quiet as it seemed. Terrible summer heat, a mysterious child, a deathly illness, and dark stirrings in the Far North hearken the winds of a rising

Storm, as storm that will change the face of Shalkan—and the lives of Brendys and his family—forever. . . .

The Flame and the Shadow – *Release not the Fire, 'til death is nigh* . . . With nowhere else to turn, Brendys takes up his crown and becomes a Prince of Gildea, governing the newly rebuilt city of Trost Keep. After an eight year peace, the Black Shadow of Thanatos falls across the entirety of Milhavior, heralding the Deathlord's return to the Mortal Realm and the revelation of the Heir of Ascon. Brendys and his companions must gather together the Alliance of the Free Kindreds—Men, Elves, Dwarves, and the hidden Saereni—to make one last stand against the Darkness. . . .

Other Science Fiction and Fantasy Books from RudderHaven

Tolkien: Roncevaux, Ethandune, and Middle-earth – Of Myths and Legends and the Creative Muse (Douglas Rudder)

The RudderHaven Science fiction and Fantasy Anthology I – Unexpected Meetings, Chance Encounters and First Contacts (C. K. Deatherage, Douglas Rudder, S. L. Rudder, Paula Welker)

The RudderHaven Science fiction and Fantasy Anthology II – Epiphanies and Revelations (C. K. Deatherage, Becca Lynn Rudder, Douglas Rudder, S. L. Rudder, B. David Spicer, Paula Welker)

The RudderHaven Science fiction and Fantasy Anthology III – Lost and Found (C. K. Deatherage, C. S. Marks, Becca Lynn Rudder, Douglas Rudder, S. L. Rudder, B. David Spicer)

Tales with a Twist (C. K. Deatherage, Larry D. Rudder, B. David Spicer)

Waysmeet: Poems and Tales of Fantasy and Wonder – Oogles and dragons, fairies and foundlings (C. K. Deatherage)

The Shadow of the Bear – Frontier fantasy set in the Dakota Territory (Larry D. Rudder)

www.ingramcontent.com/pod-product-compliance
Lightning Source LLC
Chambersburg PA
CBHW051839170626
46807CB00003B/1251